MW00412141

LADY ABIGALE'S WAGER

BRIDES OF SOMERSET BOOK THREE

KAREN LYNNE

Lady Abigale's Wager

Brides of Somerset Book Three

Copyright © 2019 by Karen Evelyn.

All rights reserved. No part of this publication may be reproduced, distributed, or transmitted in any form or by any means, including photocopying, recording, or other electronic or mechanical methods, except for the use of brief quotations in a book review, without the prior written consent from the author. For more information, address the author at:

karen@karenlynneauthor.com

This book is a work of fiction. Any references to historical events, real people, or real places are used fictitiously. Any likeness to any person, living or dead, is purely coincidental. Characters and storyline are products of the author's imagination.

OTHER BOOKS BY KAREN LYNNE

Brides of Somerset Series:

The Earl's Reluctant Bride

Courting Eliza

Lady Abigale's Wager

Isabella's Promise

Holiday Bride

Taming Sophia

Join my reader's group and enjoy updates for new books and little bits of tidbits on 19th-century history.

CHAPTER ONE

*L*ady Abigale was used to getting her way, but it was nearing the end of her third Season in London, and her father, Sir George, was concerned for her and felt she should have been married by now. It wasn't for lack of suitors that Abby hadn't "stuck," as they say. She had turned down two young men who had wished to propose already this Season. A fact she kept to herself.

Abby threw her bonnet on the side table and entered the parlor of her father's London townhome. A spring shower hung wet in the air, cutting short her morning ride in the park. It was just as well; she was growing tired of the daily visits from suitors who left her feeling weary.

If her father had just let her go to Bath for the Season. She had been writing to her friend Isabella, who lived in Bristol and was enjoying the Bath Season. She had hoped to enjoy the smaller community with Isabella, where she could develop more intimate friendships.

Aunt Lucy looked up from her stitching when Abby entered the room. Abby dropped onto the settee next to her aunt, brushing a damp curl out of her face. Aunt Lucy, her father's sister, had been her chaperone and companion ever since her mother died. She was a most affectionate, indulgent aunt, doting and loving, although she too was beginning to lose patience with her.

"Abby, dear, you're damp. Is that why you're back so soon?"

"I'm afraid it began to drizzle just as we entered the park. Thank heavens, I had my parasol. I think my dress can be dried without any damage." Abby attempted to brush the drops from her skirt before she gave up. Betsy, her maid, would bring the dress back to life. It really was fortuitous that they had been caught in the shower. Her companion, though sweet, in a boyish, innocent way, was dull and stirred no passion as a young lady would hope.

"I think you ordered that rain on purpose, Abby, just to get out from riding with your new beau."

Her brother, William, startled her. She hadn't seen him sitting in the corner, his face buried in the London Post. He lowered the paper just enough to stare at her, shaking his head.

Abby's eyes drilled into his. "Mr. Wyler is not my beau."

"Well, he could be if you would give him a chance." William continued to stare at his sister, giving her a knowing look.

"Mr. Wyler does not stir my emotions."

"Stir your emotions?" Her brother laughed. "Abby, everybody stirs your emotions. You're the most excitable female I've ever come across. If you keep this up, I wager you'll be a spinster by next Season just like your friend, Miss Underwood."

"Josephine is not a spinster; she's an independent woman."

"An independent spinster, no doubt," William egged her on. "Mark my word, Abby. If you keep this up, in the next year or two, gentlemen will begin to avoid you."

Abby clutched the arms of the chair as she maintained her temper. "You will see, William. I will take that wager and prove to you that I am capable of finding a husband. A husband that will suit *me,* not you or father." She stood, flouncing out of the room, her damp skirts sticking to her legs. She could hear her aunt reprimanding William as she made her escape.

"You know you will push her into doing something rash by your teasing, William."

Abby made her way to her bedchamber, where Betsy helped her out of her damp clothing. A hot bath would set her to rights. How dare her brother insinuate that she was changeable. She deserved a husband whom she had a passion for. Didn't she?

William had found his love two Seasons back. Her dear friend, Eliza, and he had fallen in love and married, and she knew they loved each other deeply. She was beginning to think that it was not possible for her to find love. The gentlemen she had met these past few Seasons were either too old or too young, tied to their mothers, and unable to think for themselves. They sparked no emotion, Abby wanted to feel something for her husband. So far, her father hadn't pushed her to marry anyone, but she didn't know how long his patience would hold.

Abby spent the morning riding in Hyde Park with Miss Josephine Underwood, taking advantage of the cool morning. They managed their horses along the serpentine, avoiding the footpaths. A groom followed at a discreet distance at the insistence of her father.

It was a clear day, and the rain had abated, making the ride enjoyable. She enjoyed her time with Miss Underwood. Josephine was a self-proclaimed spinster at the ripe old age of twenty-eight. Her parents had died and left her enough money to be independent. Abby deemed herself fortunate Josephine allowed her to be friends and to call her by her given name. Miss Underwood didn't suffer the fair sex's company often, preferring more mature acquaintances. She was taller than average, and her sharp eyes looking down her straight nose could quell any silly miss in an instant. Josephine was going to Bath for the summer and had invited Abby to come as her guest.

"I have found a house in Bath." Josephine shifted the reins and turned her mount, avoiding the children who ran through the grass as their nannies gossiped amongst themselves, turning their heads every so often to check on their charges.

"So soon?" Abby asked in surprise for Josephine had just decided to go to the country a couple of weeks past.

"Yes, I was fortunate a family left suddenly without giving notice, and my man snapped it up. It's a very upscale address in the Royal Crescent, number 20. Have you talked to your father about staying with me this summer?"

Abby shook her head. "I have been waiting for the right moment. This has to be handled delicately. He is still peeved at me for discouraging Mr. Thomas."

Josephine laughed. "I understand, and the invitation stands. I will be leaving at the end of the week before the summer heat sets in. Send me word of your decision, but I warn you, I keep myself busy with charitable work, and it can be quite dull."

"It will be a change from the parties that fill our days in London," Abby complained. "But I am sure I shall find a way to get to Bath."

Abby waved goodbye as she and Josephine emerged from the park gate and promised to send word. Abby headed towards her father's townhouse, still early as hawkers readied their carts, preparing to sell for the day. Nannies were already bringing their charges for a romp in the park before the crowds of ladies and gentlemen took their daily strolls.

A groom took Abby's mount, and she entered the front door. She could hear her father in the breakfast parlor with her Aunt Lucy. Climbing the stairs to her room for a quick freshening up before she joined them, she decided this morning was as good a time as any to broach the subject. She knew her father loved her, but could be stern. Taking a deep breath, running her hands down the front of her skirt, she entered the breakfast room.

"Abby, dear," her aunt's eyes brightened, "did you have a good ride?"

"Oh, I did. It was lovely." Abby sat and placed a napkin in her lap. She reached for a triangle of toast and buttered it. A footman poured her a cup of tea while she helped herself to a boiled egg and began to crack it, avoiding her father's eyes. Keeping her voice light, she said before biting into her toast, "Miss Underwood has invited me to stay with her in Bath this summer."

"Oh." Her Aunt Lucy looked up, blinking.

"Bath, why would you want to visit Bath? We've been over this." Her father laid his paper down on the table, raising his eyes to her. "You haven't managed to catch a husband here in London with thousands of people. Why would Bath be any different?"

Abby opened her mouth to respond when her aunt coughed. "Abby, why don't you let your father and I talk about this?" She gave her a knowing look, signaling Abby was dismissed.

Abby thought it a good idea. Finishing her egg, she stuffed the last bite of toast in her mouth, wiped her hands, and stood. Giving her aunt a nod, she quickly left the room, closing the door behind her, leaving just a crack. What was Aunt Lucy up to? She leaned her ear towards the door. Would her aunt support her with this invitation?

"Lucy, what was that about?" her father huffed.

"George, why do you insist on provoking your daughter so? I see no reason why Abby can't go and visit her friend in Bath this summer. You won't even be home most of the summer."

"William and Eliza are taking good care of the estate. Why should I drag myself back to the country?" Sir George defended himself.

"Exactly, how do you think Abby feels? Both her friends, Susan and Eliza, are married now. She has nobody else close to her age. It would do her good to go to Bath. If you're worried about her, I will contact Eliza's aunt, Mrs. Notley, in Bristol. I hear she's taken her niece to Bath for the Season."

"You won't be going with her?" Father's voice became alarmed.

"Abby will reach her majority this summer. I feel no need to go with her to Bath. There will be plenty of escorts, and she will have her maid with her. Betsy is a sensible girl."

Abby heard a cough. She turned her head to see the butler staring at her, a frown on his face. She lifted her finger to her lips and bent closer to the door. The butler raised his eyes to the ceiling and continued down the hall.

She couldn't believe Aunt Lucy was championing her cause. Her heart sped up in anticipation of going to Bath, *finally*.

"What do we know about this Miss Underwood?" her father continued. "I'm concerned that she might be a bad influence on Abby."

"You mean Abby may become a spinster, like myself." Aunt Lucy had raised her voice. It carried a slight edge.

"Lucy, I didn't mean..." Her father's voice softened.

"Never you mind. If you must know, Mr. Albert is spending time with me. Now that Abby is reaching her majority, I would like to take some time for myself."

"It's not nice to eavesdrop." A soft breath blew against her ear. Jumping back, her hand flew to her chest. William stood behind her, a stern look on his face as he tapped his foot.

"When it concerns me, it is," she threw back at him, tossing her head.

He reached for her elbow and pulled her forward. "Come, Abby, walk me to the door."

A footman was loading bags onto the back of William's curricle. "You're leaving?"

"Yes, my business is done here, and I'd like to get back to my wife. Eliza has been managing the estate for a month now. It's time I returned to her and my boy."

Abby kicked her toe against the stones as William checked his horses. "William, did you know Mr. Albert was spending time with Aunt Lucy?"

"He is? Well, good for them." William turned to adjust his luggage.

Frustrated, Abby slapped her hand against her skirt. "Is that all you have to say? What if Aunt Lucy leaves us?"

He turned to look at her. "I think it's time Aunt Lucy found a little companionship of her own. She's been taking care of us for a long time. You should worry about our wager," he advised. "I shall be thinking of what you will owe me when you lose." He leaned down and tweaked her cheek. Abby swatted at his hand.

"You know I like a challenge, William, so don't think you'll win this one." She watched him climb into his curricle. He tipped his hat as he moved into the street. Shaking her head, she entered the house again. Knowing when to leave the fight with someone else, Abby retired to her room and left Aunt Lucy to convince her father.

Abby had not thought of going to Bath without the companionship of her aunt. She had enjoyed the affection and kindness of her company for the past sixteen years. Her mother died when Abby was at a tender age. The only motherly affection she remembered had come from her aunt.

Not being a selfish creature, Abby was happy her aunt might find a place of her own. Mr. Albert was a man of exceptionally good character, good fortune, and a sensible age for Aunt Lucy.

CHAPTER TWO

*S*ir Andrew Pulteney, the fifth Baronet of Bath, was ready to go home to his Bathwick estate. It had been a trying session. They had been unable to get a bill to clarify the Slave Trade Act of 1807, which Sir George Phelips had brought forward through the House of Commons for legislation. The bill had been bouncing around the house for the last several years. It seemed no one wanted to commit, and so the debates continued.

Andrew entered White's Club on 37 James Street, a copy of the Edinburgh tucked under his arm. He found members of Parliament discussing the bills that were currently before the House.

Sir George welcomed him to a seat. "Sir Andrew, we were just discussing that if Jenkinson would call a vote, we might get the Slave Trade Act expanded throughout the British Empire."

Andrew sat, putting his paper aside. "You may try, Sir George, but I believe we don't have enough votes yet. We've been debating this for the last two sessions."

"You're probably right." Sir George's brow wrinkled. "We only have a month left before we break. I guess it's too much to hope for a positive conclusion."

"Yes, I agree, so I've decided to head home. I haven't seen my son for a while." Andrew pushed the paper toward Sir George. "Did you hear the Pentrich rising has been stopped? They hung the ringleaders at the Derby ghoul."

Sir George reached for the paper, shaking his head. "The Luddites broke up lace-making machines in Loughborough in February. I don't agree with their tactics, but I understand the recession has hit the working class hard."

"I believe it will take time. The war has only ended these past two years, it's painful to accept change, especially when it affects your livelihood," Sir Andrew replied.

"You reside in Bath, do you not?" Sir George asked.

"I do, in the parish of Bathwick, where I have an estate."

Sir George sat and pondered as if something substantial weighed on his mind. "My daughter, Lady Abigale, is visiting Bath this summer with a friend, Miss Underwood. She will be leaving within the week. My sister believes it will be good for her, but I have my concerns."

Andrew recalled the young miss he'd seen several Seasons ago. Like many of the young debutantes, he tended to avoid them. "We have many visitors during the summer. They take the waters and avoid the hot London summer."

"Yes. My sister has made all the arguments, but I would feel reassured if you could check on her, nothing formal . . . Just if you happen to see her in society, it will put my mind at ease as she is reaching her majority this summer."

While Andrew certainly didn't want to play nursemaid, he tried to remember what the lady looked like. Blonde, pretty face, full of giggles like the rest of her kind. He should make an excuse, but he respected Sir George, and as a father, he could sympathize with his concern. He nodded as he found himself agreeing. "Give me her address, and I will see what I can do."

He would make a courtesy call to the girl and set Sir George's mind at ease. Then it would be done, and he could turn to his duties at home. He hadn't remarried after his wife died shortly after the birth of their son. She was docile and met his needs. It hadn't been a love match, but he did not need to love his wife. It was less complicated that way.

He hadn't given much thought to it lately, but it was probably time to think of remarrying for the sake of his son. A mature lady would be best, someone who didn't expect anything from him, but someone who could guide his young son until he was old enough to be sent to school. Then his wife could do as she pleased. He had plenty of money, that wasn't a problem as long as his wife didn't interfere with his comfortable life.

Sir George was true to his word and sent the address of where his daughter would be staying, along with the direction of Mrs. Notley of Bristol, who could be notified if need be.

Miss Underwood, 20 Royal Crescent Bath. The residence was in a good part of town, which gave him pause. He was not about to get caught up in Bath society and hoped he would not regret helping Sir George.

Abby woke up to sunshine and a happy countenance. Aunt Lucy had somehow convinced her father to let her spend the summer in Bath. Miss Josephine Underwood had left three days before and promised to have the house set up by the time Abby arrived.

Arrangements had been made for her to travel with Mrs. Packett and her two daughters. Not the best traveling with the Packett sisters, for they tended to quarrel amongst themselves. It could be tedious to be trapped in a coach together. But she wouldn't complain. Surely, she could endure two days of travel when the reward was a summer in Bath.

Betsy had finished her packing, and they were to leave on the morning coach. Aunt Lucy had given her strict instructions and reminded her to behave like a lady. She promised she would come for a visit later in the summer. Mrs. Notley of Bristol had been informed, and Abby could expect an invitation.

Mrs. Packett and her daughters met Abby at the station and made their greetings. "Lady Abigale, it was good of your father to allow us to accompany you as far as Bath."

"Oh no, Mrs. Packett, I am most grateful for you to escort me." Abby gave her a slight nod and a pretty smile.

The sisters giggled, and Miss Millicent nudged her sister. "Lady Abigale, I have brought a guide book and look forward to pointing out the interesting historical sights."

Abby smiled. "As we are going to be together for the next two days, please call me Abby."

"Oh, lovely, and you may call me Liz, and my sister is called Milly by her friends."

Liz gave Abby a wide smile before heading to their coach, where the luggage and trunks had been loaded. No sooner had they left and turned towards the Tyburn Turnpike when Liz, who sat by a window, began to watch the scenery, keeping her place in her book. An hour later they passed through the village of Southall.

"Southall supports a weekly market on Thursdays where they sell cattle, which are the best in Middlesex, except those held in Smithfield," Liz informed them.

"Cattle, *cattle*! What do we care about cattle?" Milly screeched.

"Cattle are vital, especially to Southall," her sister argued.

Their mother, Mrs. Packett, had dozed off soon after they left London. Abby was amazed that she could sleep through all the bumping and swaying of the coach and the constant arguments of her daughters.

Abby turned to the window, watching the scenery go by. A small church made of flint and brick came into view. It was a neat structure with a tower at its west end. It looked to have been built hundreds of years before but must have been well cared for by the villagers. Memories of the vicarage back home and its chapel came to mind. The church of Saint Catherine, it had been built in the twelfth century and updated through the centuries. Her ancestors were buried in the adjoining cemetery.

The coach stopped, bringing her out of her thoughts. She welcomed the rest and a short break. Betsy followed Abby through the inn to a room set up for female travelers. She freshened up, then followed her nose; the smell of fresh pastries wafted through the air. She bought two buns with ham and cheese and five apple tarts that were still warm from the oven.

The crunch of wheels could be heard on the cobblestones. The door swung open, and a tall man in a dark cloak pushed his way through, brushing past Abby. He turned, his sharp eyes gazing down at her face before moving past. Abby's skin tingled, she took notice of his commanding manner. Was he someone important?

She moved outside, where a black lacquered coach rounded the corner of the inn. Walking to the edge of the building, she peered in awe as it was an exceptionally built carriage with a gold and red B monogrammed on the door. Four brilliant black horses pulled the sleek vehicle. Surely it was designed for speed Abby thought.

Her coach driver signaled their departure, and she hurried aboard. Abby shared her meal with Betsy and wiped her hands on the napkin before pulling out an apple tart and handing one to each of the occupants.

"Thank you, Lady Abigale, for your consideration," Mrs. Packett acknowledged as she took one of the apple tarts. Her daughters parroted their mother's thanks before hastily devouring the treat.

Abby took a taste of the apple tart and closed her eyes, slowly savoring each bite. It reminded her of home. Mrs. Baxter made the best pastries. She was the housekeeper and cook at Fyne Court, Lady Susan's childhood home. Mrs. Baxter was a jolly person who enjoyed teaching Abby to make apple tarts.

"It's a way to a man's heart," she would say. "Even the finest lady should be able to cook a few treats." She didn't mind Abby spending time in the kitchen with her. It was an activity she would never have been allowed to do at her father's home at Montacute. Their cook was persnickety about his kitchen.

Abby tried to rest, but the noise the sisters were making prevented any meaningful sleep. When the coach pulled into the inn for the night, Abby's nerves were stretched to their limits, although Betsy seemed to be in good spirits. How was she going to make it through another day? The Old Crown Coaching Inn, the sign read. She needed some food and a respite from the constant chatter of the Packett girls.

They retired to their rooms after dining. Abby and Betsy were led to a small room facing the front of the inn while Mrs. Packett and her daughters slept in the bedchamber toward the back.

Restless, Abby soon slipped out with Betsy for a short walk under the full moon when the jingle of harnesses brought her attention to the same sleek black coach she had seen earlier pull into the inn. Its impressive owner stepped out and mumbled directions to the grooms before going into the Old Crown. Abby nudged her maid, "Betsy, go find who owns the coach and where they are bound."

Betsy scampered off to talk to the grooms. Appearing back shortly, she informed her mistress, "Tis Sir Andrew Pulteney, the fifth Baronet of Bath. His man says he's headed home to Bath this very evening. They're only stopping for a few hours to rest the horses. With the light of the full moon, he bragged they should make it by dawn."

Abby could believe it with those prime horses. Her mind formed an idea as she and her maid walked to and fro in front of the inn, careful to stay in the light of the lamps. "Betsy, how would you like to make it to Bath tonight and not have to listen to the Packett sisters?"

"Would be a blessing to my ears, my lady," Betsy said, "but what have you planned?"

They returned to their room as Abby explained to Betsy what they needed to do. They had a servant carefully bring their luggage back down and set it on the corner of the building so as not to be seen through the windows.

Abby had removed a black cloak from her trunk and wrapped it around her. Pulling the hood over her hair, she sat down and waited for Sir Andrew to finish his business, then Betsy went into action.

CHAPTER THREE

"*P*lease, sir." A petite girl looked up at Andrew as he was paying the innkeeper. He looked into her eyes and listened as she continued. "Your man tells us you are headed to Bath this evening."

"Yes," Andrew answered, keeping his voice firm. He looked at her with suspicion.

"My mistress, an elderly widow, is on her way to Bath. She has received news from her son that her grandson is very sick and wishes to see her for fear he will die. She fears if she waits for the morning coach, she may not be there on time. We would ask for a small favor. If you could give us a ride, it would be greatly appreciated."

Andrew could feel his insides tightening. He preferred his solitude. "Where is your mistress?"

"She is just outside, sir, waiting with her luggage."

Andrew stepped to the door and noticed a dark figure wrapped in a cloak sitting on a trunk of excellent quality.

"You look to be of quality, sir, and we feel with your escort, we would be safely delivered to Bath by morning." The young miss gave him a pleading look.

As Andrew contemplated the situation, compassion took over, and he walked towards the widow.

"Sir." The miss stopped him. "She prefers her solitude and is very tired from this day's journey. We won't be any trouble. If you would just say yay or nay, that will do."

Andrew could feel his ire rising. He wanted this trip to be done with and hated unnecessary complications. His life ran smoothly, and that was how he liked it, but he could not just leave a widow sitting alone in the dark when he had the means to help.

"Very well. I'll have my man load your luggage, and you may help your mistress into the coach."

"Oh, thank you, sir." The miss responded excitedly. "I shall inform my mistress."

Abby couldn't believe their luck as she slowly ascended the steps, trying to appear as feeble as possible. She kept her head ducked under her hood while she seated herself in the far corner, tucking her cloak further around her.

Betsy sat next to her as they listened to Sir Andrew

shout orders to his men. He was soon sitting opposite them in the coach. He tapped his cane up on the roof. The coach lurched forward, and they were on their way into the darkness.

Abby laid her head against the side of the carriage and feigned sleep, willing him not to speak to her. She must have dozed off for soon Betsy was giving her a nudge, and she opened her eyes. She could just see the light of dawn coming through the carriage window.

"If you would give me your address, we can set you down at your door," Sir Andrew offered.

"Oh, we have given our address to your man," Betsy spoke up.

Abby stole a glance from under her hood, watching as Sir Andrew talked to Betsy. He had a look of confusion as if he wanted to say something. But then his face cleared, and he held his tongue. His well-dressed attire of dark colors was not of the latest fashion but of good quality. He'd been leafing through a stack of papers by his side, reading as the light of morning came through the windows.

Abby looked up at the impressive facade, and her heart leaped as the coach stopped in front of 20 Royal Crescent. A smile appeared on her lips as she lowered the hood of her cloak. Finally, she made it safely to Bath.

Sir Andrew's men were efficient. As soon as the coach stopped, the door was opened, and the step lowered. The lady's companion descended with Andrew following. The men were already unloading the luggage and carrying them to the door of number 20 Royal Crescent. His brows knit together as he realized the address was the same given to him by Sir George.

He looked into the carriage while the matron looked out the window. She lowered the hood of her cape, and golden curls fell across her shoulders, turning her smiling face toward him. Crystal blue eyes met his in the early light of dawn. Lady Abigale's familiar face had matured into a distinctive beauty. A stirring deep inside began to rise, but before he could utter a word, she moved towards him, stepping out of the carriage.

"Sir Andrew, we are so grateful to you for delivering us safely to Bath. I hope we can repay you for your kindness." Her clear melodic voice resonated through him.

She was ascending the steps of the home before he could respond. A butler opened the door, his clear voice could be heard in the street. "Miss Phelips, we have been expecting you." Lady Abigale stepped through the door and was gone.

Andrew continued to stare at the door of number twenty. She knew his name, he thought as he slowly climbed into his carriage and sank into the seat. The little minx—, he'd been duped. What had he gotten himself into?

CHAPTER FOUR

"*T*he mistress is still asleep," the butler informed Abby. "The housekeeper will show you to your room." The help seemed to be efficient, Abby thought as she followed the housekeeper up a flight of stairs.

Abby was so excited, she didn't know if she could rest, but Abby knew she needed to. It had been a long trip. The bumping of the coach and the constant bickering of the Packett sisters had taken its toll, and she could feel her muscles beginning to stiffen.

Betsy helped her undress, then Abby laid her head on the pillow. She must have fallen asleep immediately, for she remembered nothing until Betsy gently woke her.

"Miss Underwood is going to town and wanted to know if you would join her?"

Betsy sat a small tray with a hot bun and tea on the

small table by her bed. Abby sprang from the bed and looked out the window. A bright morning with no rain, good. She reached for some gowns in the wardrobe. Throwing a few on the bed, searching for a walking dress, she began slipping one on, hardly waiting for Betsy to help her. Abby devoured the bun before leaving her maid to clean the mess.

Josephine was tying on her bonnet when Abby descended the stairs. "Today is market day. I enjoy the walk and picking out fresh produce, I thought you'd like to join me."

Abby agreed, eager to explore the city. They stopped first at the baker where Josephine bought half a dozen Sally Lunn buns and a dozen Sydney tea rolls.

Abby struggled to keep up with Josephine, whose long legs outpaced her. They made a right on High Street and found the market on the left. Delighted with the sights and smells, Abby purchased winter apples, which she determined would make tasty apple tarts. Gladdened it had turned into a pleasant day, Abby and Josephine stopped at the tea room and enjoyed a delightful luncheon before returning home.

"Lady Abigale, a gentleman stopped by and left his card," the butler informed them before relieving them of their parcels and bags, carting them off to the kitchen.

Abby retrieved the card from the side table in the hall. "Sir Andrew Pulteney," she read. Abby began to feel guilty at having deceived him. What had he meant by calling on her? Abby handed the card to Josephine.

"Sir Andrew Pulteney? I am surprised he has called. Are you acquainted with him?" Josephine asked, handing his card back to Abby.

"No, I am not– I met him on the road while we were traveling here." Abby dared not to mention her deception. "Sir Andrew was kind enough to give us a ride from Farlington to complete our journey. I will not tell how tedious the first part of the trip was, caged up in a traveling coach with Mrs. Packett's daughters," Abby confessed.

"Oh, yes, I am familiar with the girls. They are fine if you can get them alone, but together they, well…" Josephine smiled, nodding.

"I will not feel bad that I left them. My father paid their fare, and I did leave Mrs. Packett a note so she shouldn't worry," Abby tried to convince herself.

"If Sir Andrew has made a special call to you, I am impressed. He is the leading citizen here in Bath. Old family. He represents the borough of Bathwick in the House of Commons."

That bit of information did not make Abby feel better. If he was a member of Parliament, that meant he knew her father. What luck to have picked him for her trickery. Abby would not think about it, for she determined to enjoy herself and refused to let it spoil her trip. Abby followed Josephine to the back parlor which was situated very nicely with a view of the back gardens.

"I would like to go to the workhouse this afternoon,"

Josephine said. "You are welcome to stay at home or come with me."

"The workhouse?" Abby was curious. "What will you do at the workhouse?"

"I would like to find a cook. They train young women in domestic service, and I would just as well hire from the workhouse rather than an agency. I have been very pleased with them in the past."

Abby brightened. "I think that is an excellent idea, and I would love to go with you." Abby thought about Fyne Court, which housed young ladies in need. She would like to see how the workhouses did their training.

"Are you not worried about references?"

Josephine waved her hand and scoffed. "References, no, I have a pretty good sense of measuring a person. Besides, the workhouse has records that will fill me in on the women's history. Most of the workers don't have references. Many have fallen on hard times through no fault of their own. With a little help, they can be back to supporting themselves. We should leave for the workhouse at three o'clock. I will leave you for now as I need to confer with the housekeeper before we leave."

Abby walked over to the small desk by the window in search of some paper. She wanted to write a letter to Miss Isabella Dalton informing her of her arrival in town and where she could be found.

Abby finished two more letters to Susan and Eliza, regaling them with her adventures of riding with the

Packett sisters on their journey, made even more tedious by Miss Millicent complaining of her sister's monologue of the attractions along the way. Mrs. Packett slept the whole way, oblivious to her argumentative daughters. Satisfied, Abby sealed the letters and left them on the tray in the hall, along with the shillings, for the butler to post.

Refreshed and shod in her walking boots, Abby and Josephine left the Crescent on foot to visit the workhouse. Betsy followed, armed with a parasol just in case of a summer shower. At half-past the hour, following the London Road, they arrived at the Walcot parish church where an old workhouse was located on the right side of the road. Abby looked up at the simple building made of red brick, which sported three stories.

The matron was pleased with Josephine's arrival and led them through the women's parlor, where many women were gathered and working on sewing projects. The matron proudly described their programs and how they helped train women in different trades. The young people would be trained to go into service, she informed them. They were led out to the back courtyard where young girls played on the grass. A red brick bakehouse stood at the far corner.

Abby sat on a bench at the corner of the courtyard to

observe the children at play while Josephine followed the matron into the bakehouse.

"My lady, this does not look like any workhouse I have heard of," Betsy said, taking a seat on the bench by her mistress.

"Where have you seen a workhouse before, Betsy?"

"My cousin in London told us about them, terrible places, they are houses of squalor. Not a place you would like to go."

The courtyard was surrounded by stone walls, Abby could hear the yelling of children's voices over the enclosure. She suspected it was the boys as the matron had said that the men and women were kept separate.

Sir Andrew had paid a call to the Crescent, but the ladies were out shopping the butler informed him. He left his card. Irritation bubbled up inside as Andrew climbed into his curricle. This was becoming a chore he didn't want to deal with. Andrew flicked the reins and headed to Harrington's. He had things to get done today before he went home to spend time with his young son.

His irritation at Lady Abigale was subsiding, though he was still curious as to why she pulled that prank on him yesterday. He should let the matter rest. He could keep an eye on her from a distance. If she got herself into any more trouble, he would let Sir George know.

He entered the club, finding the gentleman he was

looking for. Earlier that year, the city had passed a
resolution to allocate funds for a new church in
Bathwick, and a thousand pounds were earmarked for a
new workhouse. Surely by now, a firm had been hired to
draw up the plans.

Satisfied with what he had learned, he ate before
leaving to talk with the solicitors. But first, he wanted
to visit Walcot workhouse. Walking into the foyer, he
noted the cleanliness of the place. He could hear
children playing in the back courtyard. It was a stark
contrast to the workhouses he had seen in London.
The city was expanding, and Bath needed more
facilities.

The matron entered the room. "My Lord," she
curtsied, "what can we do for you today?"

"I'd like to speak with the director, Mr. Beechum."

"If you'll just wait here, my lord, I will let him know
you are here." She led him into a room off to the side,
closing the door behind him.

Andrew laid his hat on the chair and followed the
sound of the children to windows that looked out onto
the back courtyard. Young girls ran and played. They
were dressed in neat uniforms with little white aprons. A
young girl dragging a ragged doll approached two
ladies, seated on a bench by the edge of the courtyard.
It was the maid who had approached him at Farlington,
requesting a ride for her mistress. She was quite the

actress, for she had quite convinced him of her mistress's plight.

Annoyance rose as he thought how two young misses duped him into giving them a ride. Didn't Lady Abigale know how dangerous it was to accept rides from strange gentlemen? No wonder her father had asked him to check on her.

Lady Abigale smiled at the young girl when a ball flew by and hit her skirt. She laughed then, picking up the ball, she stood and tossed it back to the group of girls, giving them a wave of her hand. She leaned down to talk to the young girl who had put a thumb in her mouth.

A simple bonnet framed lady Abigale's face while blonde curls fell around it, softening the look. Andrew noted her hat was void of the fripperies so many of the ladies insisted on wearing to the point of ridiculousness. He wondered how they could keep such contraptions on their heads. Her dress had a simple, delicate lace surrounding the neck and just two flounces along the edge of the skirt. It flowed across her soft curves. She had matured since the last time he had seen her.

"My lord," the matron said as she opened the door, "the director will be here directly. May I get you some tea?"

Andrew shook his head as he turned his eyes from the window. "No, thank you. Can you tell me why Lady Abigale is here?"

The matron came to the window and followed his

direction. "Oh, yes, the lady is with Miss Underwood."
The matron brightened. "Miss Underwood is here to
hire a cook from our women. We so appreciate Miss
Underwood, for she comes here to hire help whenever
she's in town."

Andrew mused, watching the scene before him. The
matron left him, closing the door behind her.

Lady Abigale continued to talk with the young girl.
He was amazed that she had no qualms talking to the
lower class. Most young ladies avoided them or
pretended they weren't there. Andrew was beginning to
think lady Abigale was an unusual woman.

CHAPTER FIVE

*J*osephine and Abby returned home after a pleasant visit in which the matron of Walcot had promised to send several applicants to the Crescent for Josephine to interview the next day.

"The butler and housekeeper have been providing simple fare for our meals, but I can't help to be happy to have a cook," Josephine said.

"I'm sure you will find someone," Abby replied, "but I should like to take advantage and go out to the market with Betsy. I would like to make some pastries with the winter apples I bought."

She would make some apple tarts and send them to Sir Andrew, thanking him for his hospitality.

Josephine's eyebrows raised. "Did I hear you right that you were going to bake? I have never heard of such a thing from a lady before."

Abby clapped her hands together in delight. "Oh, yes, Josephine. I can bake, thanks to Lady Susan's housekeeper at Fyne Court. I do tolerably well in the kitchen. I hope your new cook will tolerate me rumbling around occasionally."

"I shall put that on the requirement list," Josephine teased her.

Abby left the house early the next morning with Betsy in tow for the housekeeper's feathers had been ruffled when she found that Josephine was going to interview for the position of cook on her own rather than letting the housekeeper manage them. Applicants had started to arrive and were directed by the butler to sit in the hallway where chairs had been placed. Josephine was to interview each one separately in her office, and the line was growing as Abby made her way out the door.

Abby had gone to the larder the night before and made a list of the supplies she would need. She was thankful her father was generous with her allowance. He had credit set up with the local bank should she need any funds, but her pin money was plenty to pay for the goods she planned to buy this day.

The smells and sounds of the market delighted Abby as she made her way through the stalls. She would make arrangements for the larger purchases to be delivered to the house. She found hard candies for the children in the workhouse and stalls full of colorful dried fruits of every kind. Little brown nuggets were labeled *dates*. She'd heard of the fruit but had never tasted one.

"Dates, my lady," the stall keeper said. "They come from India into the port of Bristol. Would you like to taste one?" He handed her one of the brown nuggets.

Abby bit into the soft, sweet morsel. A rich honey flavor exploded in her mouth. Her eyes widened as she smiled at the merchant. "I'll take one pound."

Her goods had been delivered by the time Abby returned to the townhouse. Applicants were gone from the hall, and Abby found Josephine in the back parlor.

"You will be happy to hear our cook will be here tomorrow," Josephine informed her.

"I hope she isn't fastidious about who is in her kitchen," Abbey replied. "I have bought some marvelous dates." Abby held up her package. "We shall have some with our tea."

Abby scooted off to the kitchen to organize her supplies. The winter apples sat in a bowl on the table. She picked one up and smelled. She would make the apple tarts before the new cook arrived.

Andrew entered the dining room to see the butler had laid out the evening post. Taking a seat, he arranged the paper as the butler poured his tea.

"My lord." The butler cleared his throat. "Lady

Abigale has sent a box of pastries addressed to the servants. She states that she made them for your staff as a thank you. She has also included a box for you. I have taken the liberty of giving you one with your evening tea, along with the note."

Andrew lowered the paper and stared at the pastry by his cup. There was indeed a note addressed to him.

His brow wrinkled. "Did you say Lady Abigale made them?"

"That is what her note stated, my lord, to thank you for the service you provided."

He laid down his paper and picked up the plate, turning it from side to side. A small apple tart with cinnamon, sugar, and walnuts sprinkled on top sat neatly on top of a napkin. It was still warm; he took a sniff.

"The staff sends their thanks. Will you tell Lady Abigale next time you call, my lord, that the staff has thoroughly enjoyed them?" His butler bowed and moved to the side.

Andrew laid the plate down, picked up his knife and fork, and slowly sliced a piece and lifted it to his lips, the taste of sweet-tart apples delighted his tongue, a bit of honey. He looked down at the delicacy and poked it with his fork. Small pieces of dates had been added. He took a few more bites, surprised at how well it went with his tea. He couldn't believe that Lady Abigale had made the tarts on her own. Miss Underwood must have hired a cook.

Leaning back in his chair, he wiped the crumbs from

his lips with his napkin and picked up the note. His name was written in neat floral handwriting, scrolled across the front. He broke the seal.

Sir Andrew,

I told you I would find a way to thank you for your kind service in delivering me to Bath. I sincerely apologize for any deceit I may have dealt you.

I found these beautiful winter apples at the market the other day and thought they would make tasty pastries.

As they are the only things I know how to bake, I hope you and your staff enjoy them. Our cook is coming later, and I thought it prudent to make them before she arrived. You know how servants can be when you invade their domain.

I received the card you kindly left and deeply regret having missed you. Please do not feel any further obligation to call. As you can see, everything has turned out for the best.

Sincerely,

Lady Abigale Phelips

Unbelievable, Andrew reread the letter. He was being dismissed by a little chit of a girl.

CHAPTER SIX

*A*bby received a card from Mrs. Notley, they were to call on Friday and invited her to visit the pump room. Abby found Josephine in the back parlor. "Mrs. Notley is coming to town on Friday. She has invited me to the pump room."

"You should try the waters once while you're here. The waters are nasty, and I don't know that they do any good. You'll find the older set there during the day, and the younger set comes later," Josephine told her.

"Will you come with us?" Abby asked.

"I have my women's auxiliary meeting that day. Do not worry about me," Josephine said. "Enjoy your friends. I want you to do as you please this summer. I won't bore you with my projects."

"I would not call your projects boring, Josephine." Abby laughed. "I should like to see the pump room and taste the waters at least once."

The new cook settled into the kitchen, providing regular meals. The staff began to run smoothly as they adjusted to Josephine's social schedule. She had started a women's club, meeting here at number 20, so by the time Mrs. Notley came on Friday, Abby was ready to get out and away from the activity.

"Mrs. Notley." Abby greeted the ladies and showed them into the parlor. "I must introduce you to Miss Underwood, who has been so gracious to let me stay with her."

"Yes, Lady Abigale, and you will be pleased that I have brought your dear friend, Miss Isabella, along with my niece, Miss Joanne, whom you know from home."

Mrs. Notley and the ladies followed Abby into the parlor. Abby's eyes brightened. "Miss Isabella, I am so happy you were able to come." Abby moved forward as she greeted Isabella and hooked her arm.

"Let us sit. Josephine will be in shortly," Abby informed them. "Joanne, it's good to see you as well. I hope you're enjoying your stay with your aunt."

Joanne's shy eyes watched Abby. "Yes, we are having a perfect time. My aunt is very generous, and we have been rather busy."

Mrs. Notley looked at Joanne with loving eyes as she gave her a pat. "I have enjoyed having you. Your sister, Eliza, married before I could give her a Season. Not that I'm complaining." She raised her hands. "I am very happy for her."

Abby introduced Josephine when she came into the

parlor. "You will find Miss Underwood very progressive, Mrs. Notley. She has been here but a fortnight and already is organizing the ladies club to supply things for the new workhouse that is being built in Bathwick."

Mrs. Notley turned to Josephine, and a conversation began about the new workhouse.

"You must tell me your opinion about the pump room. I have heard a lot about it, but I've never been there. What does the water taste like?" Abby asked Isabella and Joanne.

Joanne wrinkled her nose. "It certainly tastes different. I think you're better to bathe in it than to drink it."

"That may be true. I have heard some say rheumatism is relieved by soaking in the mineral pools," Isabella said.

"We don't really go there for the water. There are a tea room, an assembly room, and a game room where you may always find a game of cards. Mrs. Notley loves her whist," Joanne said.

"Girls." Mrs. Notley rose from her seat. "Shall we be on our way?"

The pump room consisted of a large assembly room filled with patrons milling about. Conversing and promenading around, they made a circle of the perimeter, occasionally stopping for conversation as they met acquaintances. A highly decorated gentleman in bright livery served water from a stone fountain and little glass cups at the side of the room.

"It isn't so crowded now," Isabella said as she and Abby walked into the pump room. "It's very crowded during the season, but they've thinned out now that summer is here."

"Let us taste the water first, then we can visit." Isabella led her to the fountain. The gentleman handed her a cup with about four ounces of water. Abby gave him fourpence as the sign directed, fishing it out from her reticule hanging from a chain on her arm.

Abby followed Isabella away from the fountain. "Are you going to drink the water?"

Isabella shook her head and giggled. "I have had enough water this season."

Abby sniffed. It smelled of sulfur, although it was clear. It warmed her hand. Daring to take a sip, she scrunched her nose.

"It's best to drink it all at once." Isabella gave her encouragement.

Abby took another drink, gasping as she finished. "It tastes like gunpowder." She took a handkerchief from her bag and held it to her mouth.

"It's the minerals," Isabella said, giggling.

"I don't know how anyone can drink this." Abby looked around at all the patrons milling about, sipping on their cups.

"Yes," Isabella agreed. "I would much rather bathe in it."

The ladies circled the room several times, Isabella pointing out various persons of interest. A small orchestra played music in the gallery as people continued to converse over the strains, creating quite a hum of noise and only stopping to clap at the end of each song before a new one began.

The room was warm, and after an hour, Abby's head began to hurt. "Isabella, would you like to take a walk with me? I need to get some fresh air."

"Mrs. Notley, Isabella, and I would like to walk into town. Can we meet you back at the townhouse in a few hours?" Abby asked.

Mrs. Notley looked from the group of ladies that surrounded her, nodding her approval.

The fresh air of the outdoors was a relief as Abby opened her parasol and took a deep breath. "That's much better. I don't know how the crowds can handle the smell and the humidity."

"It's not so bad. In the winter, the crowds are much larger." Isabella laughed.

"I would like to revisit the Walcot workhouse. I bought some candies for the girls while I was shopping yesterday, and I think they would enjoy them."

"You visited the Walcott workhouse?" Isabella seemed surprised.

"Miss Underwood and I visited the week I came to town. She was looking to hire a cook. She found one, and an excellent cook she has turned out to be."

Abby entwined her arm with Isabella's as they

walked down the street. "Mrs. Randall doesn't even scold me for coming into the kitchen. You must tell me, Isabella, how your Season went. Have you found a particular gentleman?"

Isabella shook her head. "I have had several that I like very much, but nothing has come of them. I fear that I am destined to be a spinster. If I choose a gentleman my parents do not approve of, my dowry will be withheld. So, here you are, seeing me enjoying another Season."

"I am determined to find a husband before I return home. For William has bet that I shall become a spinster just because I've turned down a few gentlemen. But I am determined to find someone I like, for we will be married for a very long time."

Within half an hour, they were entering the Walcot workhouse. The matron approached with a smile and greeted them. "Lady Abigale, it's good to see you again. How is Mrs. Randall doing?"

"Miss Underwood is very pleased with her work," Abby was happy to inform her.

"I'm so glad. What can I do for you today?"

"I have brought some candies for the girls." Abby pulled out a bag from her purse. "I hoped you wouldn't mind, but I thought they would enjoy a treat."

"How kind of you. Yes, the girls would enjoy it very much. They get so little of those here. They should be coming out to play for a short period. You may wait in the courtyard until they come."

Abby found the bench where she had sat before and waited with Isabella.

"You are so like Eliza," Isabella said. "You both do such unusual things for ladies of your class."

"What things?"

"You know, visiting little girls at the workhouse, and Eliza dragged me to the circulating library in Bristol to learn about abolitionists." Isabella reached down and grabbed a twig from the ground, twirling it between her fingers.

"I don't think it's so unusual. Miss Underwood is organizing the women's club as we speak."

"Yes, and you are a group of strong women. I wish I dared to be more independent." Isabella snapped the twig into pieces before dropping them onto the ground.

Abby wasn't sure what to say as she watched her friend. She had always been independent. Her family was blessed with money and the ability to increase it. She knew not everyone was so fortunate. Abby knew many girls like Isabella, whose futures were dependent upon their parents because of their lack of fortunes.

She reached over and covered Isabella's hand, giving it a squeeze.

"Well, I shall not ponder on things I cannot change. How is Sam?" Isabella laughed.

Abby brightened. Sam was a little black boy her brother, William, bought in Bristol for Eliza's wedding present. Eliza was concerned about the little boy because his owner mistreated him.

"Sam is not so little anymore. He is free and happily running around the estate. He works at Lady Susan's Fyne Court, the lady's academy for gentlewomen. He gets wages and attends school with the village children."

"I'm so happy to hear that." Isabella brightened.

Happy voices of children could be heard as the girls filed out into the courtyard. Abby stood as the little girl she had seen before came towards her, a thumb in her mouth, dragging her rag-doll by the arm. Abby opened her bag of candy and offered a piece to the child. She readily grabbed the offering and put it in her mouth.

The candy had been distributed, and the girls wandered off to play.

Abby turned. Sir Andrew was striding across the grass towards them. "Oh, no," she mumbled, "here comes trouble."

Isabella turned to see Sir Andrew.

CHAPTER SEVEN

*a*ndrew was just finishing a meeting with the director of the Walcot workhouse. When the sound of laughter came from the courtyard, signaling the children were at play, he stepped to the window, surprised to see two young ladies handing something to the children clambering around them.

A small girl dragging a tattered rag doll stood near Lady Abigale. Miss Dalton stood by her side, engaged in the children. He recognized her from several functions he had attended last Season. He believed Miss Dalton was from Bristol, just down the road.

Lady Abigale looked like a fresh spring flower, dressed in a simple gown of sea green with small dotted flowers sprinkled across the bodice and pink silk ribbon flowing from her trim waist.

His mouth watered, still remembering the apple tarts she supposedly made. He still had his doubts about that.

She had won over his staff, and they hadn't even met her.

"Is there anything I can do, Sir Andrew?" the matron asked.

"I noticed Lady Abigale out in the courtyard with the children. She's come for another visit, I see."

The matron beamed. "Oh, yes, it seems Lady Abigale was intrigued by the children and returned today to bring them candy. I thought it was a very nice gesture."

Sir Andrew moved towards the courtyard. He was still peeved at her note but determined to pay his respects nonetheless, and this time, he would not be put off so quickly.

The young girls ran away back to their games. Lady Abigale met his eyes as he neared, and her face froze. A frown showing on her lips, she nudged her companion. Miss Dalton turned, and her eyes widened. He remembered seeing her at several events last Season. They whispered among themselves as he approached.

Miss Dalton had the same coloring as Lady Abigale. They both were stunning. He was curious as to why neither of them was married. They had both been out several years now. He stopped a few feet in front of them and gave a slight bow. They watched, waiting for him to speak. Strange, most young ladies usually fell all over him, hardly giving him room to talk.

"Lady Abigale, I just finished a meeting with the director when I noticed the two of you out in the courtyard. I understand you were giving candies to the girls."

Lady Abigale turned to the girls, then back to him, a slow smile touched her lips. "Yes, Sir Andrew, I thought they would enjoy some candies."

"Do you always go around bestowing treats on citizens of our fair town?"

"Sir?" Abby replied, confusion in her eyes.

"My staff thanks you for the delicious apple tarts you sent us," Sir Andrew reminded her.

A bright smile crossed Lady Abigale's face. "Oh, yes, I am glad they enjoyed them."

Miss Dalton looked between them as they carried on this conversation.

"Miss Dalton, it's good to see you again. Lady Abigale sent us pastries, thanking me for rescuing her from Farlington and giving her and her maid a ride into Bath."

Lady Abigale had the decency to blush as she wrapped her arm around Miss Dalton's. "Sir Andrew, I am most thankful for your help that evening. You need not bother any further for my welfare. Miss Dalton and I were just leaving." She moved to step around him.

"But Lady Abigale, I would not think of leaving you unescorted in our fair city. Your *father*, Sir George, and I are colleagues. He would want me to make sure you were well treated. I would hate to give him any bad news about your welfare."

His meaning was not lost on Lady Abigale as she

gave him a meaningful stare, a challenge in her eyes as her facial muscles tightened. She reached for her parasol on the bench. He could feel the tension as she tapped it against her skirt, almost as if she wanted to hit him with it. So, she had a temper. She was probably used to getting her own way. Spoiled, like most young ladies from wealthy families.

"Miss Dalton, are you with your parents in town?" Andrew asked.

"I am accompanied by Mrs. Notley of Bristol and her niece, Miss Grant."

Sir Andrew withdrew his card and handed it to Miss Dalton. "I would be most honored if Lady Abigale and your party would join me tomorrow evening at the Theatre Royal. My box has room for everyone. Shall I see your party there at eight o'clock?"

Miss Dalton stared at the card and then back to Sir Andrew. "Thank you, my lord. I am sure we will be able to make it."

With a slight tip of his head, he turned and left the courtyard before Lady Abigale could protest. He had Lady Abigale's attention at the mention of her father. Retrieving his hat from the lobby, he stepped out of the workhouse, satisfied. He had seen the challenge in her eyes. It would be a most interesting night at the theatre.

Abby watched Sir Andrew leave the courtyard. He
didn't even look back. That man had a way of bringing
up her ire, and they barely knew each other. A blast of
fresh air surged over her face as she and Isabella entered
the street, lifting her parasol over her head and cooling
her temper. Sir Andrew was nowhere in sight as they
made their way back to the Crescent.

"Isabella, why did you agree that we would attend
the theatre with Sir Andrew?"

"Abby, Sir Andrew Pulteney is the wealthiest and
most influential citizen in Bath. He is the most sought-
after bachelor. He does you a great honor by singling
you out. You don't say no to a man in his position."

"Why do you say he does me a great honor? He
invited all of us to attend the theatre."

"Because he has seen me all these past Seasons and
has never given me a second look. I saw the way he
looked at you. It was you he was inviting. We were
included only as a formality."

She knew Sir Andrew was doing her no honor by his
invitation to the theatre. He made it a point by
mentioning her father as a threat. What was he up to?

"I think Sir Andrew is seeking revenge on me for
tricking him for a ride to Bath," Abby confessed.

"Abby, what do you mean, tricking him?" Isabella
watched her closely.

Abby sighed. "You must promise to tell nobody."

"I promise," Isabella breathed.

Abby confessed all about that night in Farlington

when she and Betsy finagled a ride to Bath from Sir Andrew that late night.

"Oh, Abby!" Isabella's eyes grew wide. "Were you not afraid you could have been..." Isabella looked around. "Ravished?" she whispered.

"Ravished—I had Betsy with me, and besides, he thought I was an old widow."

"Well," Isabella sighed, "you are either extremely brave or a complete fool."

Probably a little of both, Abby thought as she reached for Isabella's arm.

"As you say, Isabella." Abby brightened. "Nevertheless, we shall endeavor to have an enjoyable evening at the theatre tomorrow. What do you believe we are going to see?"

"We will ask Mrs. Notley what talents we shall enjoy. They are usually quite good, as I've heard some plays go on to perform on the London stages." Isabella followed Abby's lead.

When they returned to the Crescent, Miss Underwood was out. "May we have some refreshments brought to us in the drawing room?" Abby asked the butler. "And ask if Mrs. Randall will bring us some lemonade as well."

No sooner had Abby and Isabella taken off their bonnets than the butler announced, "Mrs. Notley and Miss Grant to see you."

Mrs. Notley came waltzing into the drawing room, trailed by Miss Grant. "Girls, I am glad to see you here.

We had a lovely walk here on foot and could do with some refreshment. I saw the tray being brought down the hall as we entered."

Abby smiled at the sight of Mrs. Notley's slightly flushed face, but she appeared quite robust for a woman of her age. It wasn't but a few minutes until the door opened, and the tea cart was wheeled in. Abby played hostess in Miss Underwood's absence.

"Mrs. Notley, Sir Andrew Pulteney, has invited our group to the Theatre Royale tomorrow evening." Isabella handed her the card Sir Andrew had given her.

"Sir Andrew," Mrs. Notley murmured, studying the card. "This is certainly unexpected and quite an honor." She smiled as she handed the card back to Isabella. "Sir Andrew does not usually escort young ladies to public functions."

"That is what I was just telling Lady Abigale." Isabella turned to Abby, acknowledging what she said was true.

Abby restrained a sigh. "I'm sure Sir Andrew is just paying his respects out of honor to my father, Sir George, as they are contemporaries in Parliament. I wouldn't be surprised if my father asked him to watch out for me."

Mrs. Notley gave a hearty laugh as she put down her teacup. "Yes, my dear, I'm sure he may have. I received a letter from your Aunt Lucy, instructing me to take good care of you."

Abby's heart warmed, thinking of her Aunt Lucy.

"Yes, but that's different. You will not stifle my enjoyment this summer. My sister-in-law, Lady Eliza, tells me how good you were to her."

"Oh, yes," Miss Joanne spoke up. "Aunt Notley is wonderful and great fun."

Mrs. Notley laughed. "Well, my dear girls, I am pleased that you approve of me. Of course, we will accept Sir Andrew's invitation."

"He has requested us to meet him at the Theatre Royale at eight tomorrow evening," Isabella informed Mrs. Notley.

"Being seen in Sir Andrew's company will be very helpful for your chances of attracting attention. The *right* attention," Mrs. Notley emphasized.

It appeared her Aunt Lucy had warned Mrs. Notley of Abby's impulsiveness. She was determined to be on her best behavior.

"Isabella and I were wondering what play we shall see at the theatre tomorrow," Abby asked.

"I believe it is a comic sketch called 'The Honeymoon, or How to Rule a Wife.' It will be followed by a performance by the clown Grimaldi. We are quite fortunate he will be here for two weeks before he moves on to another city."

"That sounds entertaining, much better than a tragedy," Abby said.

"I agree," Mrs. Notley said. "I would much rather see a comedy than a tragedy. We are staying at our house in Bath at 27 Queen Square. We would love to have you come tomorrow and stay for a week. If Miss Underwood could spare you, of course."

"Oh, yes," Isabella gushed, "it would be ever so nice to have you stay with us."

Abby blinked in surprise. "Well, let me speak with Miss Underwood. As I've only been here a week . . ."

"That will be fine," Mrs. Notley said. "Do not worry; just send me word in the morning whether we shall expect you or not." Mrs. Notley rose, and they made their goodbyes until the next day.

Abby was surprised at Miss Underwood's willingness to let her spend time with Mrs. Notley and her party. After dinner, Abby and Miss Underwood took a promenade in the park across from the Crescent. Although it wasn't hot, just humid, the cooling temperatures of the evening brought everybody out.

A lively card party ensued with a group of Miss Underwood's friends, and by ten o'clock, Abby retired, leaving the group to their boisterous conversations.

Mrs. Notley sent a carriage early the next morning for Abby. Isabella smiled from the carriage window as she greeted her friend.

"I am so glad you're staying with us this week. We have a hectic week ahead. Over breakfast this morning, Mrs. Notley said if we are seen with Sir Andrew this evening, it will open up some good matrimonial prospects."

"I daresay I can't understand how being seen at the theatre with an old man can help our prospects," Abby replied, still feeling a little peeved at Sir Andrew for taking advantage of her behavior. She felt terrible about the way she handled herself, but he was rubbing it in in a very ungentlemanly fashion.

The carriage came to a stop as the wheels scraped along the cobblestones. The door was opened by the groom, and Abby descended. Followed by Isabella, they climbed the steps to Mrs. Notley's home. Abby turned to view the area; across the street stood a park, a pleasant place to spend the morning, she thought.

The door opened, and they were admitted by the butler. Her luggage was already being delivered upstairs as the housekeeper directed the footman up the twisting staircase with elegant elaborately carved balusters.

"What do you mean, an old man?" Isabella asked as she took Abby's arm in hers and guided them towards the back of the house.

"Do you not think Sir Andrew old?" Abby replied a little sheepishly.

"No, I do not. Sir Andrew is but one and thirty, and the son is but yet two."

"He is married, then?" Great, Abby thought.

"Not anymore. Sir Andrew's wife died shortly after giving birth to his son. He has yet to remarry. Although many a lady has tried to snag him, he has avoided their attempts."

Mrs. Notley and Joanne were in the drawing room when they entered. "Lady Abigale, so glad you are here; we have a rather busy day ahead."

"Mrs. Notley, would you please call me Abby? Lady Abigale is so awkward among friends."

Mrs. Notley's eyes twinkled. She smiled and agreed. "Has the housekeeper delivered your luggage to your room and settled your maid?"

"Yes, I believe so. The housekeeper was going up the stairs before we came in here," Abby said.

"Very good. First, we shall go to the bun shop and enjoy breakfast. Then a walk in the park to see everyone and finish up with some shopping and luncheon before we shall return home to rest before the theatre." Mrs. Notley drew the girls out into the street, setting a brisk pace with Joanne by her side.

"Isabella, is Mrs. Notley always this energetic?" Abby asked.

"Oh, yes, I believe she has the energy of two of us," Isabella whispered.

Abby giggled. She could believe it, and it made her happy that Aunt Lucy and she became friends.

CHAPTER EIGHT

*S*ir Andrew adjusted his cravat in the mirror. He spent the morning with his son, followed by planning the annual house party. Well, his housekeeper and steward had organized the party, Andrew just checked them and gave his approval. They had been handling the party since he could remember. His father had started it as a way to give back to the citizens, and they looked forward to it every year.

"My lord, could we at least update the color of your coat?" His valet brushed lint from his shoulders.

"What is wrong with the color? You don't like black?" Andrew pulled on the collar of his coat, turning to examine himself in the mirror. "It gives me a mature and dignified bearing. Just as one should who represents his burough in the House of Commons."

"Yes, sir, but you are not so very old that you could

wear a lighter shade of grey with a Clarence blue velvet collar and a dark green waistcoat," his valet suggested.

"It sounds like you've been paying attention to Ackerman's fashion prints."

"Exactly, sir. It is my job to keep you looking your best." His valet turned to put his brush away before picking up Andrew's hat and handing it to him, brows arched.

"I will take that into consideration, Baley." Andrew had not cared whether he dressed fashionably since his son was born. With his standing in society, he had never had to worry about pleasing the *ton*. There were more pressing matters to consider in his life without worrying about the cut of his coat.

He thought about Lady Abigale and her impish grin in the carriage that night. He couldn't get her out of his mind, and it was driving him to distraction. Never had a woman frustrated him, intrigued him, or kept him guessing like she did, continuing to push him away. He was determined to figure her out and put his mind to rest. She was interrupting his well-ordered life.

Andrew found himself pacing the lobby of the Theatre Royale, checking his fab watch when suddenly his party appeared through the crowd.

Mrs. Notley's flushed face smiled up at him. "Sir Andrew, I hope we haven't kept you waiting? The walk was quite invigorating, but we found ourselves maneuvering between the crowds."

"Forgive me. I should have sent a carriage." Sir

Andrew returned his watch to his pocket and observed the three ladies trailing behind her. They made a pretty picture in their evening wear.

Lady Abigale stood out in the simplicity of her gown of white crepe over satin, which was extremely becoming to her shape. The only ornamentation was crepe draped along the hemline, trimmed with bunches of red roses and a transparent shawl of ruby thrown over her shoulders.

Andrew recalled his valet's conversation as he tugged on his dull, dove grey waistcoat. Annoyed that he cared, he offered his arm to Mrs. Notley and escorted the ladies to his box amongst plumes of feathers and highly decorated ladies.

"That was not necessary, Sir Andrew, as I could have brought our carriage, but the crowds and the carriage jams can keep you waiting in a long line. So, you see, it was much easier to walk as we are not far from here," Mrs. Notley informed him.

He agreed as he remembered the effort his driver had taken to get him here. Andrew was determined he would see them home.

Curious glances inspected them as he settled the ladies in his box. Mrs. Notley sat on the end with her niece next to her, and him on the other side with Lady Abigale, and Miss Isabella in the middle. It had been a long time since he had attended the theatre with guests. The ladies leaned over, watching the audience below while whispering and sharing giggles amongst themselves.

Lady Abigale turned towards him. The most dazzling smile lit her face, causing his chest to constrict. "Sir Andrew, do you like a comedy?" Her eyes glistened.

Andrew watched her expectant eyes as the gaslight glistened across her face. "I like a good drama," he admitted.

She laughed outright, and the melodic sound spread throughout the booth. "I knew it." She giggled, and her eyes continued to twinkle. "A stuffy, mature man that you are, I guessed it. You probably love a tragedy mixed in with your drama."

His eyes widened. He couldn't have been more surprised had the lady slapped him. Stuffy? Mature? He wanted to lash out at her at that moment. "My lady, I am not as old as you may think."

Her eyes continued to glisten in the lamplight as a smile played about her lips. "I have offended you. Do you not take it so? Maybe if you would dress a little more—youthful, more— fashionable?" Her brows lifted.

"And what is wrong with my dress?" He had always prided himself on his sober attire, and he felt a little piqued. Because of his youth, he had to work extra hard in the House of Commons to gain the respect needed to get his bills passed, and it had worked. He was finally able to do some good for his borough that he represented here in Bath.

"For one thing, your cravat is too low, the points of your collar could be a little higher, and a little color in your waistcoat would not hurt." An impish grin played across her face.

His brows furrowed with a look that quelled most people. "Lady Abigale, I begin to understand why you have not acquired a husband, with a tongue like that."

Her gloved hand flew to her mouth, covering her smile as she suppressed a laugh, and ducked her head. She looked at him from under her lashes. "You are right, Sir Andrew. My Aunt Lucy is constantly trying to get me to curb my tongue."

He felt a prick of guilt. Lady Abigale had made him lose control. He shouldn't have spoken to her that way. Even with her bad manners, he should have remained a gentleman.

She dropped her hand and lifted her head. Her playful grin returned. She lowered her voice so only he could hear. "Because of your invitation to the theatre this evening, I am told I should have floods of attention, for which I do mean to acquire a husband this summer."

The music started with the Master of Ceremonies entering the stage. Lady Abigale's attention turned to the production below.

He was astounded. Lady Abigale had called him old and stuffy, corrected him on his clothing, and then admitted to using him as bait to attract a husband. Was

she really that scheming? He began to think she was
goading him on purpose.

After tonight, he was determined to wash his hands
of her. He had done his duty to Sir George, and Mrs.
Notley had taken charge of her. He could walk away,
whatever trouble Lady Abigale got herself into, she
deserved.

The play continued, and he tried to ignore her. She
took delight in the comic sketches. At the intermission,
their booth was flooded with admirers wanting to be
introduced to the ladies. He found himself annoyed as
she carried on polite conversations with the gentlemen.
She had an easy way and seemed to be able to talk to
anyone. Except him. He began making plans to visit his
tailor the next day.

CHAPTER NINE

*S*unday morning, Abby and her friends had a light breakfast before attending church at the Bath Abbey. King Edgar the first, King of England, had been crowned on this site, and every king since had followed with their coronation being held here. Abby was awed by the history this structure held as she listened to the service performed by the bishop.

Abby and Isabella made their way through the parishioners into the sunshine when the services ended.

"We must come back for a tour of the cathedral," Abby suggested. She would love to hear more of the abbey's history.

"Yes, it is quite ancient. There is much to see," Isabella agreed.

"Miss Isabella and Lady Abigale," two young gentlemen greeted them. "It is good to see you this fine Sunday morning."

Abby had recalled meeting these officers the other evening at the theatre and was trying to remember their names.

"Mr. Woodland, Mr. Tingley, that is very kind of you," Isabella greeted them.

"Lady Abigale, we didn't get a chance to speak much the other evening. Are you in Bath for the entire summer?" Mr. Woodland asked.

"I am, sir." Abby paused. "I have only recently arrived. Mrs. Notley has been showing me around the city."

"We have not seen you in town before. Is this your first visit to Bath?" Mr. Tingley inquired.

"Yes, Mr. Tingley, I usually spend the Season in London, and the summer in the country."

"Ladies, are you going to the ball at the assembly hall this Tuesday?" Mr. Woodland asked.

"I do hope so. It promises to be entertaining," Mr. Tingley added.

Abby and Isabella started to laugh, nodding their heads in unison. "Yes, gentlemen, we are planning on attending," Isabella informed them.

"Then, will you both save a dance for us?" Mr. Woodland asked.

They each promised to save a dance for them. The gentlemen bowed and made their exit.

Mrs. Notley swept past. "Ladies, shall we catch the promenade in the park before luncheon? There will be lots of gentlemen to see." Joanne filed past with a few lady friends in tow, following in her aunt's wake.

Abby raised her parasol and, entwining her arm with Isabella's, they proceeded to follow Mrs. Notley to the park.

"Well, Isabella, shall we promenade in the park and see how many more gentlemen will request a dance? You were certainly right about Sir Andrew."

"Oh? In what way?"

"Why being in his company would get the attention of society. It certainly has, like bees to honey. I am determined to fall in love this summer and find a husband while we bask in his shadow."

Isabella's eyes widened. "How odd you are, Abby."

Abby turned to Isabella. "Why do you say that?

"You just say, you're going to fall in love and find a husband, as simple as that?" Isabella laughed. "I find most gentlemen are looking for a wife that will bring something, status or wealth, to the marriage. As I have neither, I'm beginning to wonder if I will ever find a satisfactory marriage."

Abby touched Isabella's sleeve as she turned toward her. "Isabella, you mustn't get discouraged. As pretty as you are, I know you will find someone. Why my friend Susan was penniless, and she married an earl."

"Do you mean Lady Malmesbury? Eliza told me about her. Didn't she inherit from her grandfather, Lord Coventry?"

"Well... yes, but not before the Earl of Malmesbury

fell in love with her. He would have married her even if she hadn't inherited from her grandfather. Anything is possible. Isabella, you just have to put your mind to it. Do you believe in destiny?"

"What do you mean?"

Abby explained, "Destiny, God's will in our life. I believe there's a time and a place for everything. I feel it. I will find love this summer, and you will, too, Isabella when the time is right."

Abby had not forgotten her wager with William. She was determined. After all, she turned down many offers these past few Seasons.

The weekend had been a success. Flowers and calling cards flooded in for the three ladies of the house. Mrs. Notley sifted through the invitations, choosing which ones would be most advantageous. It was not bad, considering the height of the season had passed, and the locals were settling into the long days of summer. Abby was content and looked forward to the ball.

Sir Andrew's valet was in good spirits as he helped him dress for the evening's events. His clothes came in from his tailor, and more were to follow in the coming week.

"I told you I would consider your advice, Baley, and after thinking it over, you had a good point. It was time I updated my wardrobe. I also felt it good to support the local tradesmen."

"You have made a fine choice, my lord." His valet practically beamed as he finished tying his stiffly starched cravat. His boots had been polished to a high shine. Sir Andrew felt almost, but not quite, a dandy when his valet had finished.

He slipped into the nursery before stepping out to the ball that evening. "Papa, Papa." His son wrapped his small arms around his leg, balancing on his shiny boot. Andrew scooped the tiny figure up and wrapped him in his arms as he planted a kiss on his son's soft cheek. The child giggled and snuggled into his father's arms.

"Book, Papa, book. Read me a book," his son pleaded, and so, their nightly ritual began with Andrew reading to his son and tucking him in bed for the night. He kissed him gently before leaving the room.

Abby took extra care with her dress that evening, though she suspected the ball would be no different than those she attended in London. This time she had a purpose. She was determined to choose her husband. Betsy helped her with her hair, keeping it simple but elegant.

The promenade had gone well on Sunday. Several more gentlemen from the theatre had stopped to pay their respects and enlarged their acquaintances, securing several more dances for this evening. Abby wasn't sure if Sir Andrew would be attending, but if he did, she hoped to secure a dance, furthering her chances of securing a husband.

Abby admitted she had never put her mind to the task before, preferring to enjoy life before settling into matrimony. Twirling before the mirror, she inspected her reflection. After all, White Hart was full of men of fortune, military, and naval officers. Abby tucked her dancing slippers into her bag, and, checking her hair one last time, she swept from the room.

CHAPTER TEN

*A*ndrew ordered the carriage earlier and, by the time he slipped out of his son's door, it was time to leave for the ball. Mrs. Notley agreed to allow him to escort her and her charges. The gas lamps were just being lit when the carriage pulled up in front of the townhome.

"Sir Andrew." The butler nodded as he opened the door. "Mrs. Notley is in the parlor."

Andrew reached the parlor door when a swish of skirts was heard on the stairs. He looked up to see Lady Abigale descending, tucking slippers into her reticule.

He waited to open the door. Lady Abigale turned, making eye contact when suddenly recognition dawned, her eyes raked him from head to toe, and a slight smile played about her lips.

"Sir Andrew . . . is that you?" She slowly approached.

"Lady Abigale, I see you are dressed for the ball." He opened the parlor door, inviting her to enter. He did not want to give her the satisfaction of thinking it was because of her that he changed his attire. It had been an impulsive decision, but after seeing his valet's eagerness and delight, he was glad he did, even if Lady Abigale had pushed him to it.

She walked past him, entering the parlor. Her scent wafted through his senses as she brushed beside him, skirting through the door.

Mrs. Notley rose from a floral couch as she caught sight of him. "Sir Andrew, it is so good of you to escort us to the ball tonight."

Mrs. Notley moved past him, and he quickly opened the door again as the ladies followed her out into the hall. Lady Abigale trailed behind her, bright eyes looking up at him as she passed. "Sir Andrew," she whispered, "you look dashing this evening. I look forward to the attention you shall draw, like bees to honey." She giggled as she slid by.

What did she mean by that remark? She didn't give him a backward glance as she walked out the door. The footman was helping the ladies into the carriage when he emerged onto the street. At least she had complimented him, dashing was better than stuffy.

The young ladies shared a seat while he settled next to Mrs. Notley opposite them. Lady Abigale's eyes sparkled as she gave him an innocent grin. The assembly rooms were not far, so he gave Mrs. Notley his attention as they made their way to the ball. His driver steered the carriage into the line, and they waited their turn to disembark.

"Ladies, your dance cards should be full this evening if your number of callers this week is any indication." Mrs. Notley smiled.

"Oh, yes, it should be a very entertaining evening," Miss Isabella agreed.

"Then, I will be sure to claim a dance right away before your dance cards are full," Sir Andrew replied.

The carriage stopped, the door was opened by a groom, and he assisted the ladies out of their conveyance. Sir Andrew offered his arm to Mrs. Notley as they proceeded into the assembly hall. They were greeted at the door and given their program cards before the Master of Ceremonies welcomed them. "Sir Andrew, I am glad to see you graced our assembly."

Sir Andrew introduced them. "Mr. Ames, you know Mrs. Notley and her charges, Miss Grant, Miss Dalton, and Lady Abigale, who is visiting Bath this summer."

"Mr. Ames." Lady Abigale nodded.

They moved into the great room, lit with gas lamps installed that year. Andrew noticed it wasn't as crowded as during the Season, for which he was much relieved. A couple of gentlemen, dressed in regimentals, approached on seeing his group enter. Andrew quickly snatched Lady Abigale's card before she had a chance to attach it to her wrist. "Ladies, it seems I must claim my dances before the admiring horde's approach." He held his hand out to receive the other dance cards.

Miss Grant giggled as she removed the card from her wrist, handing it over but refusing to meet his eyes. He quickly claimed the third dance, a quadrille. A safe choice that wouldn't overly tax the young lady with his presence. He chose Miss Dalton's second dance. He thought it better to get them engaging the attention of the other gentlemen early in the evening.

A couple of ladies approached, giggling, their wide eyes assessing him before taking Miss Grant off just as the young gentlemen reached their intended targets.

"We have come to claim our dances before your cards fill," one of the gentlemen inquired.

Miss Dalton happily handed her card over to the young officers as Lady Abigale tapped her foot, waiting for him to finish with hers. Andrew relaxed, taking his time, signing his name beside the two waltzes, then handing it back to Lady Abigale.

She gave him a sweet smile, but he could feel undertones of tension before she turned her attention to the eager gentlemen.

Mrs. Notley smiled, her eyes shining. They turned and moved along the wall. "Sir Andrew, I feel you have been tasked with keeping an eye on Lady Abigale, or is there something more?" She gave him a knowing look.

"You are very perceptive." Andrew smiled. "I did agree to watch out for her as a favor to Sir George. I confess I had not expected her to be so time-consuming."

"So, it is with young ladies, I find, but you will be glad to hear that her Aunt Lucy will be arriving at the end of the week. Which will be good, for I am called home to Bristol and will be taking Miss Dalton with me."

Andrew watched Lady Abigale as swarms of young men hovered around her and Miss Dalton, their dance cards filling quickly. They were becoming very popular. It had been a while, but it was time for him to make a show of dancing with the young ladies.

He thought of his young son's need for a mother. He didn't want him to be raised by nannies as he had been. She would have to be unique, one that would take an active role in raising his son and any other children that the marriage would produce. He was probably asking too much for the ladies in his circle. He watched the group before him, or maybe he was putting obstacles in his path, resisting matrimony and the obligations that it would entail.

"I look forward to meeting Miss Phelips, Sir George's sister. I shall invite her to the annual picnic at my estate," Sir Andrew offered.

"That would be very kind of you. I'm sorry to say we will not be attending this year as my husband's business will keep us occupied." As Mrs. Notley watched the young couples dance, a small smile played about her lips.

"I am sorry to hear that, Mrs. Notley. You shall be missed."

"Mrs. Notley." A well-dressed gentleman greeted her.

"Mr. Dalton, such a pleasure to see you." Mrs. Notley greeted Isabella's brother.

"Sir Andrew." The young man gave him a bow.

"Mrs. Notley, might I impose on you for an introduction to Isabella's friend, Lady Abigale?"

"You certainly may, Mr. Dalton, but your sister Isabella could just as easily make the introduction, could she not?"

"Yes, she could, Mrs. Notley, but I would prefer the grander introduction made by you."

Mrs. Notley laughed at the young man's reply. "Sir Andrew, would you excuse us?"

He nodded as they moved off in the direction of his sister. Mr. Dalton was a nice-looking young man, although he wasn't much older than himself. He was pleasant enough when not in the company of his parents.

The music had started up from the small orchestra at the top of the room. Andrew moved on, greeting people as he went.

"Lady Abigale, I had hoped to get one of the waltzes." The young officer pouted as he viewed her dance card.

"Oh?" Abby leaned over and glanced at the card the young gentleman held for her to view. "It appears you may have to choose another unless you would like to wrestle one from Sir Andrew." She gave him her most dazzling smile to soften the blow. It worked, for he happily signed his name to two of her dances before moving on as more gentlemen appeared, asking for introductions from Miss Isabella.

Abby barely had time to think why Sir Andrew would take both of her waltzes when Mrs. Notley appeared, followed by a handsome gentleman.

"My dear Isabella, look who I have found. He has come, asking for an introduction to your friend, Lady Abigale."

"Benjamin!" Isabella's eyes widened as a well-proportioned gentleman leaned over and gave her a kiss on her cheek.

"Isabella, my dear sister, you look well. Mrs. Notley has graciously offered to introduce me to your friend." He turned a smile towards Abby.

"Lady Abigale, I would like to introduce Mr. Dalton, Isabella's brother." Mrs. Notley smiled, tapping her fan on Mr. Dalton's shoulder. "There, Mr. Dalton, I have done my duty; the rest is up to you." She gave him a nod as she moved off.

Abby found herself staring into bright blue eyes, a smile showed his dimple. He was quite handsome with the same light wavy hair, and fair skin as his sister.

"I am happy to meet you, Lady Abigale, as my sister

has talked so highly of you. May I?" he asked, reaching for her dance card.

She handed him the card and stared over his shoulder at her friend Isabella, a silent question in her eyes. Isabella shrugged her shoulders and shook her head.

"I look forward to our dance." Benjamin bowed. Returning her card, he reached over and retrieved his sister's dance card and signed his name.

"Isabella, I was sad to hear mother is calling you home, cutting short your visit with Lady Abigale."

"Oh?" Abby looked up.

"It is true. I received my mother's letter this morning. Mrs. Notley is leaving at the end of the week to return to Bristol, and I'll be going with her," Isabella said.

"I am sad to hear it, but do not despair, Isabella. Bristol is but eleven miles from here. I shall be here all summer and will find the time to come visit," Abby replied.

"I would like that." Isabella brightened.

"I think our parents would be glad to meet you. Just say the word, and I shall escort you to Bristol," Isabella's brother offered.

"That is kind of you, Mr. Dalton," Abby replied.

Mr. Woodland appeared to claim Abby's first dance, interrupting their small group. Abby watched as Isabella's brother led his sister onto the dance floor. She was surprised by his behavior as William had not thought much of him because of his neglect of Isabella.

As Abby moved onto the dance floor with her partner, she couldn't keep her mind off Sir Andrew's change in appearance, and him taking her two waltzes.

The quick steps of the Scottish dance made it challenging to converse with Mr. Woodland as she watched the gay colors of dresses swirl through the hall, enhanced by the glow from the gas lamps.

Abby contemplated her dance partner as they swung round on their turn. He was handsome enough, although his nose was a little long. Abby asked questions to get a better understanding of him. She found gentlemen enjoyed talking about themselves. Mr. Woodland made small talk about the weather as they joined the next dance.

Again, he was good-looking, but the real issue was his job as a midshipman. Could she sit at home while he went to sea for long periods? Could she fall in love with him? Probably not. She mentally checked him off her list as she was escorted to Mrs. Notley's side.

After several more dances and several more checks, she dropped several gentlemen from her list, she needed a respite.

"Mr. Easton, I fear I require a little rest. Would you mind if we sat by a cool window and talked?"

"Most certainly, Lady Abigale." Mr. Easton offered his arm, and Abby slipped her hand through, keeping her touch light. They gathered up a glass of lemonade before finding a seat by an open window.

Abby sipped the cooling liquid and flipped her fan open, waving it in front of her flushed face. "Mr. Easton, you must tell me, do you like to hunt?"

"Oh, yes, Lady Abigale," he replied as he began to give her details of his prized hunters. He was just getting warmed up to the subject when Abby noticed Sir Andrew dancing with Isabella. Her heart fluttered as it did when she first saw him at Mrs. Notley's home that evening. A strange feeling Abby had never felt before. She swallowed, pushing the feelings down inside as she turned her attention back to Mr. Easton. His face flushed with enthusiasm as he continued to talk about his dogs. She wondered what passions Sir Andrew had besides his estate and his seat in Parliament.

Abby hadn't noticed the music stop until she heard a deep voice next to her. "Lady Abigale, I believe this is my dance." She turned. Sir Andrew was at her side. Her heart thumped again as she looked into his striking eyes.

"Mr. Easton, thank you for talking with me and for the fine description of your hunting dogs." She nodded.

Taking Sir Andrew's arm, her fingers tingled with warmth as he led her onto the dance floor. He wrapped his arm around her waist, keeping air between them as the strains of the waltz began. His steps were smooth as he guided her around the room. She admired his cravat and the excellent points of his collar, dropped just below his handsome, clean-shaven face. A small dimple showed in the cleft of his chin.

Lady Abigale scrutinized his coat and cravat as she slowly lifted her eyes to his. "Do you approve?" he remarked as he cocked his brow. Most people would have shrunk from his look, but she didn't even blush as she laughed, a pleasant sound.

"Yes, wholeheartedly. As I said at Mrs. Notley's house, a vast improvement."

"Yes, I recall you said like bees to honey. From that remark, I assume you still intend to use me as bait to catch a husband?"

She lowered her eyes and at least had the courtesy to blush. "I never used the word bait."

"Yes, but you implied it."

"I do apologize. But I was a little put out at your threat to tell my father of my behavior if I didn't attend the theatre with you."

"I never said that." Sir Andrew's eyes darkened.

"Not in so many words, but it was implied. I highly suspect that my father tasked you with spying on me while I was here. You cannot blame me for taking advantage of the acquaintance."

She had a point, and he was not about to admit to keeping an eye on her as Sir George had asked.

"Sir Andrew, let us not quarrel. I know we got off to

a bad start. Can we not start over and be friends? Your acquaintance has already done the trick." She dangled her dance card before his eyes. "My dance card is full, thanks to you, and I have been checking the gentleman off my list."

"Your list?" His eyebrows raised.

"Yes, a list of qualities you want in a husband, or a wife, as in your case. You cannot tell me a gentleman doesn't have a list of qualities they want in a wife?"

"Yes," he admitted, "but Lady Abigale, I am not used to hearing it so bluntly from young ladies."

Her delightful laugh filled the air again. "You are right, Sir Andrew. But I promise you, I can hold my tongue when needed."

"Indeed." He gave her a skeptical look.

"Yes, I can, and I will prove it. Come, let us be friends so that I will not worry about you tattling to my father."

"Lady Abigale, I do not *tattle*." He gave her a stern look, softening it with a slight smile. "I agree it would be better to be friends as I fear you would be a challenging enemy."

"Wonderful. As Mrs. Notley will be leaving at the end of the week, might you help me in finding a husband?"

She never ceased to surprise him. "Lady Abigale, how can I be of help in finding you a husband? It escapes me."

CHAPTER ELEVEN

*A*bby had never danced so many dances in a row and began to wane as the night wore on. She had even suggested to sit out a few, which allowed her to rest as well as interview the current gentleman. Abby never thought picking a husband could be such a chore. If Sir Andrew would consent to help her, she knew things would go much quicker.

Mr. Dalton arrived and interrupted Abby's thoughts. "I believe this is our dance, Lady Abigale." His slight smile showed a dimple. He really was quite attractive and well-formed in his fashionable attire. She took the arm he offered, and they moved onto the dance floor where the next set of dancers lined up.

"Isabella tells me your parents are merchants and have done very well for your family."

"Yes, they are." His brow cocked in her direction.

"Do they own ships as well, Mr. Dalton?"

"No, my parents own warehouses along the waterfront in Bristol and deal with distributing imported goods."

"Oh, I see. Will you work with your parents in the business? Or will you retire a gentleman in the country to live off your parents' wealth?"

Mr. Dalton's eyes widened as he gaped at her. "Lady Abigale." He laughed, his smile returning. "You are a very forthright lady. Wouldn't you rather talk about the weather?" He bowed and swung her around, following the steps of the Lancers Quadrille before he was out of talking range.

"If this subject makes you uncomfortable, we can talk about the weather," Abby responded as he came back to her side. Concerned she had made him uncomfortable with her blunt questions, she gave him a demure smile. He was the most intriguing of her partners thus far, and she was curious at Mr. Dalton's friendly behavior towards her.

"Certainly not, Lady Abigale, but I shall hold off my answers to your questions until the dance is finished, as you are making me miss my steps."

She felt compassion for him and held her tongue for eleven minutes until the set had finished. She took his arm and walked towards her group.

"To answer your question, Lady Abigale—see? I have been quite attentive." Mr. Dalton tapped her hand with his. "My father has spent a large sum of money on my education, and he expects a return on his investment. So, I have been working with him to learn the business."

"And do you like the import business, Mr. Dalton? Or is it something that is expected of you?"

"I do not dislike it, Lady Abigale. My parents can be difficult. They are not affectionate. I disagree with the way my father does things, but what son doesn't? I may have a chance to change things in the future, one never knows." He smiled.

He walked Abby over to her aunt. "Ah, Mrs. Notley, I have returned your charge."

"Lady Abigale, I thank you for your amusing conversation. I hope that I may call on you?" Mr. Dalton bowed.

"I would like that, Mr. Dalton."

"Like what?" Isabella asked as she joined the group.

"Lady Abigale has consented to let me call on her," her brother informed his sister.

"Oh." Isabella's eyes widened as she looked between her brother and Abby.

"Do not fret, sister. I will be on my best behavior. I believe I have your next dance?" He offered his arm.

Isabella let him lead her away. Looking over her shoulder, she gave Abby a shrug.

"I believe Isabella is surprised at her brother's attention," Abby informed Mrs. Notley.

"I quite agree, and I am just as astonished as she. I can't remember when I last saw Mr. Dalton so animated."

"I confess, I like Mr. Dalton. He isn't what I expected, not from what William told me about him. Let's see if my opinion of him holds up upon further acquaintance."

"Lady Abigale." Her heart fluttered as Sir Andrew's voice resonated through her. "I am here to claim the last dance." He bowed.

"Mrs. Notley." He nodded in deference to the older woman before taking Abby's hand and leading her to the floor. His touch jolted her fingers even through her gloves. She wondered at it, for he was the only gentleman that evening to make her vibrate with these new sensations.

The music started, and Sir Andrew wrapped his arm around her waist, pulling her near. She held her breath as the sensations continued, and he began to whirl her around the ballroom. She dared to look up. He gave her a half-smile.

"Lady Abigale, I have decided to take you up on your offer to find you a husband. But only on my conditions. No, do not say anything. I will call on you this week to go over the details." He pulled her closer, causing her skin to tingle, silencing any objection she may have had. She concentrated on keeping up with his steps to avoid stumbling while the room whirled around them. His spicy scent tickled her nose, making it harder for her to keep up. Relief flooded through her as the music ended. She stepped from his embrace, and the world stopped spinning.

The party gathered their wraps and stepped into the night. Fresh air hit Abby's face, bringing her back to her senses. Sir Andrew helped her into the carriage, his touch reverberating through her. She slid to the far side of the seat, leaning her head against the door. Abby closed her eyes, blocking her view of Sir Andrew and his commanding figure. She was just tired from too much dancing, that was all.

Abby woke the next morning, sun pouring through her window. Betsy brought a tray filled with tempting delights and placed it on the small table next to the cold fireplace.

"I know you had a late night, ma'am, so I brought you a tray."

"Thank you, Betsy. I fear my head is still a little muddled from the late night."

"The tea will do you good, then, my lady."

Abby agreed. Pulling back the covers, she swung her legs over the bed and reached for her dressing gown. Slipping her feet into the slippers by her bed, Abby walked to the sitting room and splashed cold water on her face. She turned her head from side to side as she examined her reflection in the mirror. Not too bad. No dark shadows under her eyes. She reached for the brush and applied tooth powder, cleaning her teeth thoroughly.

Back in her room, she reached for her letter on her

dresser and poured a cup of tea. Snatching a sprig of parsley off her tray, she began to chew. The fresh green taste exploded in her mouth.

Taking her tea and a letter to the window seat, she settled down against a pillow, and, with the sun warming her, she re-read her aunt's letter. Aunt Lucy would be here either tomorrow or the next day, depending on the condition of the roads. The rains had stopped, so she might make better time. Abby was glad she was coming. Mrs. Notley was taking Joanne and Isabella back to Bristol at the end of the week and had offered her home for Abby and her aunt to use.

She had been bustling from place to place since she got to Bath. It would be nice to just spend the day walking in the park and getting some strawberry ice in town. Sir Andrew had not told her when he would be calling, but she was curious as to whom he would recommend. She sat back, gazing out the window. Her room faced the back of the house, where a small kitchen garden could be seen. At the end of the plot, a gardener taking advantage of the cool morning dug in the dirt below. She found herself comparing Sir Andrew to the other interested beaus.

Abby entered the parlor; a plethora of floral arrangements were scattered throughout the room. Isabella entered behind her. "It appears we were quite popular last night." She smiled. Walking towards some bouquets, she plucked a card from one of the arrangements, reading the note before taking another. "It is a shame. Just when things are getting exciting, my mother calls me home." Isabella sighed.

"We shall make the most of the next few days," Abby promised.

A maid walked into the parlor, carrying a few more bundles of flowers. "We are running out of space, my lady." The maid looked around.

"Take them to the other rooms in the house," Abby said.

"Yes, my lady." The maid left the parlor, her arms full of color.

"I would like to get a breath of air before afternoon callers begin. If the flowers are a forewarning, I think it will be a crowded afternoon." Abby linked arms with Isabella. Making their way to the hall, they collected their parasols and walked across the street into the park.

"I was surprised when I met your brother. He's not like William described him," Abby said.

"He must have been impressed by you; I have never seen him be so attentive to a female before." Isabella laughed. "Too bad I am going home. I would have liked to see if it lasts."

"It really is inconvenient when you've had so many gentlemen show interest in you to just up and leave." Abby kicked a stone across the path.

"I am used to it." Isabella sighed. "My mother sent word that she's giving a dinner party. A gentleman is attending she wants me to meet."

"We shall eat luncheon in town, then I will buy you strawberry ice as a parting gift," Abby promised.

Children's laughter caught her attention. A young boy and girl chased a ball across the lawn, reminding her of her nephew, who was just beginning to walk. The flowers were in full bloom, and dew still moistened their petals while the hum of bees could be heard as they buzzed between flowers competing for pollen.

"Abby, you're wool-gathering. Is it Sir Andrew and the waltzes last night that has you so far away?"

"Isabella!" Abby exclaimed. "I was thinking of my nephew. Do you know he is nearing two this summer?" She twirled her parasol, creating a small breeze in the humid air. "By the time I see him again, he shall be running away from the nanny and causing all kinds of mischief, I expect."

"Eliza and William must be so proud."

"They are, and I expect them to fill the house with heaps of children."

They completed a second round through the park before entering the parkway and walking toward town for their luncheon. "You know, the ladies were abuzz with gossip when we came to the ball, escorted by Sir Andrew, and he danced with Joanne and me. But he took both of your waltzes. You should have heard the whispers among the gentry. The mothers were positively jealous for their daughters."

"They would not be if they knew he was only doing it as a favor to my father. He has practically made me his ward. Why he even agreed to help me find a husband."

"You can't be serious." Isabella raised her brows. "Are you sure it is not himself looking to be your husband?"

Abby laughed out loud at the thought, then covered her mouth with her hand as she looked around. She needed to be more genteel, especially in public. "Isabella, that is absurd. I have done nothing but annoy him since we met. I promise you he only wants to keep my good reputation intact for my father's sake."

Isabella gave her a skeptical look as they reached the eatery.

"I will say, several gentlemen were put out that my waltzes were taken, but I was able to eliminate quite a few from my list. With Sir Andrew's help, I can concentrate on the few who pass the test." They were shown to a table, and Abby skimmed through the menu before giving the server her order.

Isabella shook her head. "You have a test for a potential husband? What do you do? Check off a list of attributes?"

"Well, sort of." The server brought two lemonades over ice with a sprinkling of raspberries. Moisture dripped from the frosty glasses. Abby took a sip, savoring the sweet taste. "Hm, this is delicious."

Isabella followed, agreeing it was just what they needed after their morning walk in the park.

"I hope to like my husband, and he should have a

profession or at least serve somewhere. I would hate for him to laze around, living off my inheritance. A gentleman needs to be busy doing good so that he doesn't get into mischief. Surely that is not asking too much?" Abby took a bite of her chicken.

"Yes, I agree you are very sensible. You will write and tell me all about your search?" Isabella smiled, taking a bite of her luncheon.

"Of course." Abby nodded, concentrating on her meal.

Abby watched the surrounding patrons. An elderly matron sat with her small pug, delicately feeding him tidbits from her meal. A family with three well-behaved children ate while their father read the post, and the mother fussed with the baby.

"Isabella." Abby folded her napkin and placed it on the table. Reaching in her reticule, she extracted coins to pay for the meal. "I want to take you to get the most delicious strawberry ice. Miss Underwood took me there the first week I resided with her."

She gathered her parasol, and Isabella followed, their walking boots clicking on the stone walk. They headed in the direction of the confectionary shop.

CHAPTER TWELVE

*S*ir Andrew visited his son in the nursery before attending to the business of his estate. His housekeeper and steward had the summer lawn party in hand. Invitations had been sent, and the weather looked like it may cooperate. Although the humidity was high, tents would be set up to keep the guests out of the sun.

It was a time when all classes of citizens could mix for an enjoyable day with their families. He usually invited a few guests to stay for the weekend. He decided to invite Sir George's sister and Lady Abigale.

He should have been offended by her request to help her find a husband—as he'd suspected she thought him a father figure—but instead, he'd found himself agreeing. After all, the young men he had seen flocking around her would be putty in her hands. They weren't strong enough to handle her larger-than-life personality.

And he—well, he did not feel like a father to Lady Abigale. Quite the opposite, she stirred emotions in him he had never felt before. Mostly irritation, but something else as well.

He should quit while he was ahead and move on since her aunt would be here to guide her. But for some reason, he kept coming back into her presence. She certainly wasn't dull. She would need a husband who could keep her in hand without breaking her spirit. Someone who could guide her without eating up her inheritance.

He met with his solicitor, who gave him reports on his holdings in America and his plantations in the West Indies. He would need to make a trip there soon as it had been several years, and it was imperative he visit his holdings to keep his stewards honest, and profits maximized.

Maybe he could make it a wedding trip? Lady Abigale's eyes haunted him. He must be mad. She would drive him to distraction— but what a distraction it would be. He smiled at the thought.

Abby and Isabella returned to the house at one-fifteen. She handed her parasol and shawl to a maid and noticed the silver savor on the side table filled with cards. Sir Andrew's was not among the top cards. He hadn't made an appearance today. Disappointed, she ascended the stairs to change for their afternoon visits. Betsy was waiting when Abby entered her room. Untying her ribbons, she handed her bonnet off to her maid.

"My lady, Miss Phelips arrived while you were out this morning."

Although her aunt's letter did not mention it, Abby knew why she was coming. Mrs. Packett must have written her father of her leaving them at Farlington. She didn't regret the act, for she could not have made it another day cooped up in the carriage with Mrs. Packett's cantankerous daughters. It was just her bad luck to pick Sir Andrew's conveyance.

Abby washed up and finished dressing. Returning downstairs, she could hear voices coming from the drawing room. She entered, happy to see her aunt looking so well after her journey. "Aunt Lucy, I did not expect to see you this early." Abby approached and gave her a peck on the cheek.

"We started out earlier than expected. The roads were tolerable. Mr. Albert insisted on accompanying me, so we made good time."

"Mr. Albert came with you? Alone?"

"I would not worry so much at my age, but no, dear. My maid accompanied us. Everything must be proper as an example to my niece." Her aunt smiled. Eyes twinkling, she gave Abby a knowing look.

Abby clapped her hands in delight, choosing to ignore her aunt's subtle warning. "Aunt Lucy is Mr.

Albert courting you?" Abby sat down next to her aunt, preparing to hear the whole story.

"Abby, how you go on." Her aunt blushed as she waved her hand in Abby's direction. "Let's say we are enjoying each other's company." Her smile brightened.

"I see that you and your friends have made a conquest." Her aunt changed the subject, peering around the room alight with color.

Abby followed her aunt's eyes. The maid had arranged the bouquets artfully around the drawing room. "Yes, we have been very blessed. Sir Andrew escorted us to the ball last night and danced with Joanne, Isabella, and myself, in turn, causing a sensation. We danced all night."

"Sir Andrew?" Aunt Lucy's brows raised as she turned to Mrs. Notley for confirmation.

"Yes, it is true, Lucy, Sir Andrew has been escorting the girls about town the past few weeks," Mrs. Notley replied.

Isabella entered the drawing-room. Abby stood and greeted her. "Isabella, my aunt has arrived while we were out this morning." Abby linked her arm with Isabella and brought her to stand in front of her aunt.

"Aunt Lucy, I'd like you to meet Miss Isabella Dalton."

Her aunt's eyes glazed over Isabella and took in her countenance. "Miss Dalton, it is good to meet you."

Abby sat down next to her aunt again while Isabella

bobbed a curtsy before joining them, sitting in a chair next to the sofa.

"Miss Dalton, could you be the reason Sir Andrew has been so attentive since Abby has been in town?" Aunt Lucy asked.

Isabella's eyes widened as she looked between Aunt Lucy and Mrs. Notley. "Oh, no, my lady, I assure you, Sir. Andrew has never addressed me personally until Lady Abigale came to Bath." She looked at Mrs. Notley.

"That is true," Mrs. Notley confirmed. "Our most distinguished bachelor has shown Lady Abigale much interest since she has been here. He has been kind enough to include Joanne and Isabella in his attention, which has opened up their prospects considerably, as you can see." She waved her hand around the room, indicating the flowers. "And this is just after one ball."

"I see." Aunt Lucy looked at Abby. "Well, dear, I think I'll change and rest before dinner. Come, help me." She patted Abby's hand.

Now Abby would find out the reason her aunt made this visit when she would rather stay home and be courted by Mr. Albert. Abby turned her head to see Isabella watching her leave the room, mouthing the words *good luck*.

She would need it. Although her aunt was indulgent, she had her limits and could be as stern as her father. They reached her aunt's room, where her maid had finished unpacking. Aunt Lucy let the maid help her into a comfortable dressing gown before excusing her.

Her aunt settled on the divan and fluffed some pillows before she relaxed into them, resting her feet on a plush stool.

"Abby, dear, can you guess why I have come to Bath, leaving my comfortable home to ride for days, rattling across dusty roads in this humidity?"

"Mrs. Packett—?" Abby guessed, looking down at her shoes as if suddenly interested in the pattern, unwilling to meet her aunt's gaze.

"Do you know how upset your father was when he got Mrs. Packett's letter saying you had disappeared off into the night?"

"I left Mrs. Packett a note," Abby offered, but it sounded weak even to her.

"Really, Abigale Phelips . . . I have taught you better . . . You know how dangerous it is to travel these roads between London and Bath. You could have been murdered and thrown into a ditch along the road, and we would never have been able to find you, or worse . . . no, I will not even mention it." Her aunt brushed the hair across her forehead before letting out a deep breath.

"Your father was ready to come and find you when we received a letter from Mrs. Notley, informing us that she had taken you under her wing, and Sir Andrew was making sure you were well received." Aunt Lucy's fingers trembled as she smoothed her dressing gown.

"He still may have come to drag you home,

vowing to marry you off to the first mature gentleman who would agree, had I not offered to come in his place. You have greatly inconvenienced me, Abigale. You are just fortunate Mr. Albert offered to escort me here and stay so that we might continue our acquaintance."

Abby was intelligent enough to keep her mouth closed and look repentant as her aunt continued her tirade.

"Thank heavens it was Sir Andrew who offered to bring you to Bath. Betsy was with you, I presume?"

"Yes, of course," Abby acknowledged. "He delivered us early just before dawn at Miss Underwood's. Nobody was aware of our arrival."

Her aunt took another deep breath, steadying her temper. Abby could see she was beyond frustrated as her coloring returned to normal. When she spoke again, her voice was calmer.

"Abigale, you are no longer a child running around, playing larks everywhere. You are also not an innocent seventeen-year-old debutante. Abby, you must take care. It is time you settled. I don't want you to lose your excitement for life, but it must be tempered with wisdom and maturity. I see that Sir Andrew has taken care to protect your reputation. At least that is something."

"You know Sir Andrew?"

Her aunt gave her a frosty look. She was obviously still annoyed at her behavior. "Yes, dear. Sir Andrew is a very wealthy, influential peer. He has known your father for many years."

"Why have I not met him before?" Abby asked.

"Because he does not mix with young debutantes nor mothers looking for husbands for their daughters." Her aunt gave her a look as if she should have known this.

Abby knew it, Sir Andrew was spying on her. Well, she would be on her best behavior, and he would forget she'd pulled that little prank on him. Abby would charm him with her . . . well, she would think of something.

"Abby, I must rest. Mrs. Notley has invited Sir Andrew and Mr. Dalton to dinner. She was gracious enough to include Mr. Albert. Do you think you can keep out of trouble while I rest?" Her aunt closed her eyes, dismissing her.

She turned and left before her aunt found anything else to berate her with. Abby returned to the drawing room, much chastened. She hated it when Aunt Lucy was cross with her. Abby knew she deserved it, but it was difficult to hear from someone she loved so dearly. Aunt Lucy was correct, of course. She could have come to harm. It pained her to disappoint her aunt, and she vowed to make it up to her.

Abby entered the drawing room to find Mr. Woodland seated. He quickly stood when she came into the room. "Lady Abigale." He came forward to greet her. "We were just discussing how fine the dance was last night."

"Indeed, it was, Mr. Woodland," Abby agreed, sitting next to Isabella. They continued their small talk for the next fifteen minutes until Mr. Woodland retreated. Several more gentlemen callers passed through the drawing room before it was time to dress for dinner at six, which was slightly late for dining compared to the country, but it worked well for the long summer days in the city.

CHAPTER THIRTEEN

*A*ndrew's valet was careful in his dress that evening as he prepared him for dinner at Mrs. Notley's. Baley had done his job well, brushing the last specks from his shoulders. Sir Andrew's boots had been spit-polished, his coat hugged his muscular frame, and his pants were pressed to perfection. He had no complaints about his valet, who had an excellent eye for what was fashionable without being gauche.

Letting his driver take the closed carriage in case it rained, he settled back against the seat and relaxed, although it was a short drive into town.

Mrs. Notley's butler admitted him. Taking his hat, he handed it to a footman before showing Andrew to the great room where guests had started to gather. Across the room, Lady Abigale conversed with Miss Isabella and her brother. Miss Joanne giggled softly at something

Lady Abigale said while Mr. Dalton nodded in agreement. The small group appeared comfortable.

Mrs. Notley swept over when he was announced by the butler, bringing him into a circle of adults. "Sir Andrew, I want to introduce you to a guest."

"Miss Lucy Phelips, I'd like you to meet Sir Andrew, whom you may already know from London."

"Yes." Her soft smile welcomed him. "Sir Andrew, it's good to see you."

"Miss Phelips," he said, bowing, "always a pleasure."

She turned to a mature gentleman at her side, whose soft brown eyes gazed at her tenderly. "Sir Andrew, may I introduce Mr. Albert?"

Andrew offered his hand. "Mr. Albert, I'm glad to meet you." Andrew watched Miss Phelips lay her hand gently on Mr. Albert's arm, who immediately placed his hand tenderly over hers, giving it a slight squeeze.

"Lionel, Sir Andrew serves in Parliament with my brother, Sir George."

Andrew was not immune to the tenderness these two showed each other. He remembered hearing that Sir George's sister, Miss Phelips, had seen her share of heartache in her youth and had chosen not to marry. She had moved into her brother's household when his wife died and taken over the care of Lady Abigale.

Miss Phelips leaned in a little closer and lowered her voice. "Sir Andrew, I am told we have you to thank for keeping Lady Abigale out of mischief and protecting her reputation." Miss Phelips smiled. "Her father and I are very grateful."

What could he say to this kind lady who, apparently, loved her niece deeply? He nodded, looking towards Lady Abigale. Her back was turned to him while she continued to visit with her friends. Her head bent slightly as she listened; soft yellow curls fell over her creamy neck. Turning back, Miss Phelips watched him observe her niece. A slow smile played about her lips while she turned her attention back to Mr. Albert.

Mrs. Notley announced dinner and led the group into the dining room, halting his thoughts. Although Mrs. Notley said dinner would be informal, she had put place cards by their places. "We are one gentleman short, but I think the seating arrangement has worked." Mrs. Notley preceded them into the dining room.

Andrew found himself seated on Mrs. Notley's right, with Lady Abigale next to him, followed by Mr. Dalton. Abby's aunt sat across from him on Mrs. Notley's left, with Mr. Albert next to her and Miss Isabella next to him, facing her brother at the end of the table. It was all in keeping with their rank. Andrew was glad the small table allowed them to join in each other's conversations.

The two footmen brought in the first course of soup, serving their mistress first as they made their way down each side table. "Helena, I have not seen your niece, Joanne," Lady Abigale's aunt commented.

Mrs. Notley answered, "Yes, she is visiting with her friend Lady Sophia Moore and her mother. Since we will be leaving the day after tomorrow, she wanted to spend time with them before we leave for Bristol. She will be back with us tomorrow evening."

"I'm so glad." Miss Phelips paused, her soup spoon above her bowl. "We should be able to see her, then, before you leave."

Sir Andrew ate his soup as he listened to Mr. Dalton engage Lady Abigale's attention to his right. It was apparent Mr. Dalton was interested in Lady Abigale, but Andrew wondered at his suitability as a husband. Andrew wasn't well acquainted with him.

Lady Abigale leaned over, whispering, "Sir Andrew, you're quiet this evening."

His wine glass was halfway to his lips before he slowly lowered it back to the table, giving him time to contemplate his answer to her question. He turned and observed Mr. Dalton, who was talking to his sister across the table. He lowered his voice. "I am listening and observing whether Mr. Dalton is a suitable candidate."

Lady Abigale's eyes brightened. "And what have you decided?"

"I haven't." He raised his wineglass and took a drink. "I will give you my report when I know."

"I look forward to your opinion," Lady Abigale remarked as she took a bite of her meat. Her eyes softened when they landed on her aunt across the table.

Andrew followed her direction. Her aunt leaned into Mr. Albert as he talked into her ear. Lady Abigale sighed before her attention was pulled away by Mr. Dalton.

As the meal progressed, Andrew continued to observe Miss Phelips and Mr. Albert, as they were seated directly in front of him. It appeared they were very much in love, and if they were not, they soon would be. Would Mr. Albert come up to scratch and ask for Miss Phelips' hand in marriage at this late age? And would she accept him? He wondered how it would affect Abby.

Abby? When did he start thinking of her in that way? He wondered what she would think of his son. He pushed the thought from his mind as the footmen began to clear the dishes from the table.

"Gentlemen, you're welcome to stay for a little longer and enjoy your port, or you may come with us into the drawing room." Mrs. Notley rose from her seat. The gentlemen all stood while the ladies strode out of the room. Mr. Albert and Mr. Dalton followed. Andrew sat back down as the door closed behind them. He watched the amber liquid as the footman filled his glass. He relaxed and sipped the drink, letting his head clear.

"Abby, dear, why don't you play for us?" her aunt requested.

The windows were open, letting in a cool breeze. Abby walked over to the pianoforte and sat down, then began her favorite tune. Sir Andrew had not come into the drawing room with the rest, and she wondered why. Mr. Dalton joined her on the bench, turning the pages of her sheet music while Mrs. Notley wrangled the other three into a game of cards.

"Mr. Dalton, what shall I play next?" Abby asked as they put their heads together, shuffling through the sheet music.

Sir Andrew walked through the door and settled into a high-back chair, swinging one of his shiny boots over his leg and listened. Abby could feel his presence, strong and commanding.

Mr. Dalton slid in closer as she continued to play, his leg touching hers; he leaned in as he turned the pages of her music. Though his warmth was comfortable, it held no sparks. It was like sitting next to her brother, she thought as she turned and gave him a smile.

She noticed Sir Andrew watching them as she peered over Mr. Dalton's shoulder. His eyes darkened, and a firmness settled on his lips as he gripped the arm of the chair.

The clock on the mantel chimed nine when she finished her last song and rose from the bench.

"Lady Abigale, you play very well," Mr. Dalton complimented her.

"Thank you, Mr. Dalton, I do enjoy playing." They wandered over to the card table where Abby hoped to enjoy a better view of Sir Andrew, but Mr. Dalton suddenly announced, "I must be leaving." He leaned over and, taking Abby's hand, placed a kiss on her knuckles. "I hope you will go driving with me next week, Lady Abigale."

"You will not be returning to Bristol with your sister?"

"Not for a few weeks," he admitted.

"Then I would love to go for a ride," Abby assured him.

"Delightful, I look forward to it." Mr. Dalton bowed and bid her goodnight. "Isabella, will you walk me to the door?" her brother asked.

Isabella looked at him with surprise but complied with his request. Brother and sister left the drawing room while Mr. Albert stood and took hold of Aunt Lucy's hand. "I must take my leave as well, for the hour is late. But I should be back tomorrow." Tucking her hand in his arm, they walked out of the room.

When the door closed behind them, Abby clapped her hands. "Mrs. Notley, I think Aunt Lucy is being courted."

"Yes, my dear." She laughed. "I think she is."

"I am so happy for her." Abby giggled, hardly able to contain her excitement.

"Won't you miss her if she marries?" Sir Andrew asked.

Abby turned to him, eyes wide. "Yes, of course, I will miss her, but I wouldn't want to stop her happiness.

I should see her for the holidays, I would hope, for she wouldn't live far."

Mrs. Notley patted Abby's arm," You are a good girl. I can see why Lucy is so proud of you."

Andrew cleared his throat, "Well, Mrs. Notley, thank you for dinner. I am sorry you will be missing the garden party."

Abby and Mrs. Notley walked him to the door. Aunt Lucy and Isabella watched as the other carriages left.

"Miss Phelips, an invitation to my garden party has been sent, inviting you and your niece. I hope you will accept." He bowed.

"Thank you, Sir Andrew, I'm sure we will." Her aunt smiled.

The four ladies stood at the door as the last guest, Sir Andrew, departed into the night.

It had been a lovely evening. Abby laced her arm with Isabella's and turned to ascend the stairs.

"Isabella, your last day is tomorrow. Before your return to Bristol, let's spend the day together doing something we enjoy."

Isabella nodded, keeping her head down. Abby noticed her eyes were shimmering like pools of glass. "Isabella, what is the matter?"

"It is nothing, Abby. I am fine." Isabella gave her a weak smile, but her chin trembled.

"I can certainly see that you are not fine." Abby guided Isabella to her bedchamber. "Come, let us talk about it."

Abby led her into the sitting room and lowered her onto the couch. Looking around, she snatched a handkerchief from the bureau and placed it in Isabella's hand.

Isabella nodded her thanks, unable to speak.

Betsy was preparing Abby's bedclothes in the other room. "Betsy, you may go now. I'll call you when I need you."

"Yes, my lady." Her maid quickly retreated and closed the door softly behind her.

Abby settled next to her friend, placing her hand on Isabella's.

"You were perfectly fine before you escorted your brother to the door. Did he say something to upset you? I should have words with him if he did," Abby threatened.

"Oh—, no, no," Isabella replied between sniffles. "Benjamin has been so kind to me since he met you. I would not have that ruined. He does like you, Abby."

"And I like him, too, but I will not have him causing you distress."

"My brother has not caused me distress. It's just what he said." Isabella blew her nose into Abby's handkerchief. "He warned me that my parents were planning to have me marry Mr. Stone."

"So… you do not want to marry Mr. Stone?" Abby watched Isabella try to dry her tears. Stone, the name was very plain, she thought.

Isabella shook her head as the tears started again. "He is too old for me."

"Oh, when you say old, like Sir Andrew?" Abby's eyes twinkled while trying to coax a smile out of Isabella.

Isabella chuckled between her sobs. "Oh, Abby, if only he were like Sir Andrew, but he's not. He is more like your aunt's Mr. Albert."

"Mr. Albert . . . why he's old enough to be your father!"

Isabella nodded her head vigorously as she wiped her nose. "Mr. Stone is nice enough, but I don't want to be his wife."

"Of course not." Abby patted her hand as she sat back against the couch, wondering what she could do to help. "What will you do?"

Isabella dried her tears as she finished blowing her nose then she sighed with resignation. "I suppose I will have to marry him if my parents insist."

"No, no, you shall not, Isabella. Promise me you will not marry someone you do not love and who is older, much older. You shall run away if that happens."

Isabella chuckled, her lashes still damp from her tears. "Abby, I have no friends to run to, no money, nowhere to go."

Abby sat, thinking, her mind racing. "Yes— yes, you do." She quickly stood and rushed to her desk. Pulling out some paper, she dashed off an address. Opening her desk drawer again, she pulled out a pouch and emptied the coins onto the desk, counting quickly.

She put the coins back into her pouch and folded the note and stuffed it in the bag.

Abby returned to the couch and sat next to Isabella before pressing the pouch into her hands. "If you find yourself being forced to marry someone you don't love, I want you to take this money. I have placed the address to Fyne Court. You are to come and find your way there. Promise me." Abby squeezed Isabella's hands.

"But, Abby," Isabella tried to push the bag back into Abby's hands. "I cannot take your money."

"Yes, you can, for we are like sisters, you and I. Do it for Eliza and William. They would not want you to be unhappy."

Isabella relaxed into the couch, gripping the bag to her chest.

"Promise me, Isabella, or I shall have no rest worrying about you."

Isabella looked up through her, once again, watering eyes. "I promise, Abby." She smiled. "Thank you."

"There now." Abby patted Isabella's arm. "You should like Fyne Court. Mrs. Baxter is the housekeeper and takes care of all the young ladies who find themselves in need. She taught me how to make apple tarts."

"She sounds wonderful." Isabella smiled.

"Now, tomorrow, we shall have a grand day all to ourselves. We will hire one of those sedan chairs to take us about the city and stop in and get some strawberry ice."

Isabella nodded; her tears now dry.

Abby walked Isabella back to her bedchamber and made sure she was safe before returning to her own room. Abby would have the butler notify visitors that they were not receiving tomorrow so they could enjoy the day together.

Sir Andrew met with his steward that morning, following up on the invitation to Miss Phelips and her niece. He was assured the message had been delivered that morning to Mrs. Notley's residence.

His mind at rest over that matter, he entered the playroom set up downstairs in one of the parlors. He had a desk put in so he could work while observing his son at play. A small wooden riding pony sat in the corner where the sun filtered through the window, and when opened, a breeze blew in, immersing the room with fresh air. Small wooden animals in pairs, scattered around the wooden ark of Noah, lay undisturbed on the carpet as if his son had just been there.

He sat down at his desk. Broken crayons and pencils were still scattered at the other end where his son wrote. He smiled as he pulled up some paper and dipped his quill.

Mr. Dalton, Mr. Woodland, and Mr. Tingley would be his first gentlemen to investigate. He must find out more about their character. Writing some more information for his solicitor, he sealed the letter to deliver that day. His solicitor would be able to check the integrity of these men.

Andrew checked on the progress of the party, making sure everything was in order. He felt the need to make a good impression with Lady Abigale. He hoped she approved of his estate.

CHAPTER FOURTEEN

*A*bby entered the breakfast parlor to find her
friends already there. She chose a light
breakfast of toast and fruit from the buffet and sat down
next to Isabella. She unfurled her napkin and placed it
on her lap, checking to see if Isabella survived the
night.

"I am fine, Abby," Isabella reassured her, giving her
hand a squeeze.

Abby looked into Isabella's eyes. There were no
traces of tired circles or puffiness. She appeared to be
happy. Abby relaxed and continued to eat her breakfast.

"Abby, dear, we have received an invitation from Sir
Andrew this morning for his garden party. He has
invited us to stay the weekend and has graciously
included Mr. Albert." Her aunt beamed with pleasure.

"You shall enjoy yourselves, I'm sure," Mrs. Notley
commented. "Sir Andrew's garden party is the highlight

of the summer for the citizens of Bath. The fortunate guests who are invited for the weekend enjoy his beautiful manor, which has the most exquisite gardens."

Abby's eyes brightened. "I look forward to exploring the gardens."

"I'm sorry I shall not be there, but Lucy, you must come back and stay here for as long as you wish," Mrs. Notley said.

"Helena, that is most generous, but we can find rooms at the hotel now that the season is over," Aunt Lucy replied.

"No, no, I insist. With my niece, Eliza, married to your nephew, William, we are family now. Besides, the house will just sit here empty with all these servants."

"If you put it like that, Helena, we are most grateful," her aunt replied.

"Aunt Lucy, Isabella and I are going to spend her last day together. I have notified the butler that we will not be receiving today. We are hiring a sedan chair to go about the city," Abby explained.

Aunt Lucy looked to Mrs. Notley. "It is fine, Lucy. You'll find lots of young ladies exploring the city in sedan chairs; it's very fashionable."

"Well, then, Abby, that will be fine, but I would like you to take Betsy with you."

Abby wiped her mouth and laid her napkin aside before standing. She walked over to her aunt and leaned in to give her a kiss. "Thank you, Aunt Lucy. We shall see you later this afternoon."

The afternoon flew by quickly while Isabella, Abby, and Betsy enjoyed strawberry ice and visited local museums, followed by a walk through the market gardens. By the time they arrived back to the townhouse, their feet were sore. Abby pulled a few coins from her purse and paid the sedan chair operators their agreed price. They ascended the stairs, dragging their tired feet. Abby couldn't wait to get into her room and remove her boots.

"I had a wonderful day even if my feet are tired," Isabella moaned good-heartedly. "I should be supervising the maid in packing, as we will be leaving early in the morning."

"I hope you will find time to rest before dinner," Abby said.

"I'm sure I shall." Isabella smiled, waving Abby off before departing to her bedchamber just a few doors from Abby's.

Abby untied her bonnet and threw it aside as she slouched into a comfy chair. Quickly untying her laces, she removed her boots and sat back and closed her eyes, savoring the quiet and taking a moment to rest. The door opened, and Abby could hear the splash of water as her maid entered the room. Opening her eyes, she saw Betsy set the pitcher down on the bureau and pulled a fresh bar of soap from her pocket, laying it beside the pitcher.

"I have brought fresh lavender soap and some water for you to wash up, my lady."

"Thank you, Betsy." Abby stood and let her maid

help her undress. Splashing fresh water on her face, she inhaled the scent of lavender.

"Miss Joanne has returned, and Lady Sophia and her mother, Lady Moore, will be staying for dinner. Mrs. Notley said to let you know."

Abby dried her face and went to bed. Pulling back the covers, she climbed in, yawning. "Betsy, could you wake me in an hour?"

"Yes, my lady."

Abby could hear her maid closing the door behind her. Lady Moore was from back home and seemed to know everybody's business. Maybe she had picked up some tidbits about Sir Andrew while she was here. Yawning again, Abby hoped to find out.

Dinner was a quiet affair with Mr. Albert, Lady Moore, and her daughter, Lady Sophia, as guests. Mrs. Notley's cook had provided a simple but delicious meal with soup as a first course, followed by two meat dishes with vegetables and finished with a plum pudding. The company soon retired into the drawing room. Joanne and Sophia settled at the pianoforte and began to play while the four adults sat down for a game of cards.

"Isabella, do you think I can find information on Sir Andrew Pulteney's family at the lending library?" Abby settled into a stuffed chair next to her friend.

"I should think so. What kind of things would you

like to find out?"

"Who his family is, how they came to settle in Bath. I would like to understand a little more about Sir Andrew's character."

"Are you researching to see if he's husband material?" Isabella's eyes brightened, giving Abby a teasing smile.

Abby giggled, shaking her head. She kept her eyes down and picked up some sewing beside her chair. She would not admit to Isabella the strange feelings she felt when Sir Andrew was near. "Well, he doesn't appear as old as I thought at first."

Isabella laughed. "Yes, I find he can be charming when he wants to be. And he wants to be charming to you, Abby."

Abby shook her head, refusing to make a comment. "Lady Moore, what do you know of Sir Andrew Pulteney of Bathwick?" Abby asked.

Lady Moore raised her head from her cards. She seemed surprised at the question. It did not take her long to form her opinion. "Sir Andrew is a very eligible bachelor who refuses to dance with the young ladies. Even though he attends the London Season, he ignores the ladies and spends his time with the gentlemen, talking politics. He has all the girls aflutter yet continues to disregard them, keeping himself aloof."

"My dear Lady Moore, aren't you being a little severe on Sir Andrew?" Mrs. Notley asked, laying a card on the pile.

"Oh, no, I am not, Mrs. Notley. If you could see him while he is in London, you would understand. Why he even ignores my sweet Sophia. Who could ignore such a beautiful face?" Lady Moore declared.

All eyes turned to Lady Sophia, who sat next to Joanne at the pianoforte. She looked up and smiled sweetly, batting her raven lashes.

Abby groaned inwardly, clenching her teeth as she maintained her smile. Lady Sophia was Joanne's best friend, but ever since they were little, Abby found her difficult to be around.

"But Lady Moore, what do you think of Sir Andrew's character?" Abby continued to probe.

"His character?" Lady Moore's brows arched. "Sir Andrew is wealthy, handsome, and unmarried. What more is there?"

Mrs. Notley's eyes widened at Lady Moore's declaration. Abby could tell she wanted to say something, but she held her tongue as she played out her hand. Aunt Lucy and Mr. Albert both smiled, keeping their comments to themselves.

Joanne and Sophia giggled behind their hands while Abby turned to Isabella. "I hope I find more information at the lending library," Abby whispered.

Abby hurried downstairs for breakfast the next morning. Mrs. Notley and the girls had left earlier, and only her aunt and Mr. Albert were in the breakfast room. Abby was only slightly surprised to see Mr. Albert so early, but since her aunt had arrived, he had been in constant attendance.

"Aunt Lucy," Abby asked as she filled her plate with eggs, "what time are we leaving to go to Sir Andrew's estate?"

"Noon, dear."

Abby sat next to Mr. Albert across from her aunt. Shaking out her napkin, she placed it in her lap. The footman leaned in and poured her a cup of tea.

"Aunt Lucy, I would like to go over to the lending library this morning before we leave. I will take Betsy with me. My bags are all packed and ready to be placed in the carriage."

"That only gives you a few hours, Abby." Her aunt looked concerned. "I would not want to put Sir Andrew out when he is kind enough to send a carriage."

"I promise to be back in time."

Mr. Albert lowered his paper and put his hand over Aunt Lucy's, giving it a slight squeeze. "My dear, we can always pick her up from the library on our way."

Her eyes widened, and her smile softened as she looked at Mr. Albert. "Why, that's a wonderful idea, Lionel." She turned to Abby. "We shall pick you up on the way, dear, so you may take your time."

"Thank you, Aunt Lucy, Mr. Albert." Abby quickly finished her meal and left to gather Betsy before stepping out into the sunshine. It was already beginning to get warm; the humidity was oppressive in the air. Abby raised her parasol, hoping to gather a little shade from its canopy. She wore a light cotton walking dress with a straw bonnet to stave off the heat.

It didn't take long to get to the library. It was an impressive building, made of sandstone, with its golden shade of brown and columns holding up a stone porch in the classic Roman style. As Abby entered the hallway, her boots clicked on the stone tile floor. Wooden bookshelves lined the walls with rows on both sides of the large room filled with books. Abby approached the desk where a middle-aged gentleman leaned over a ledger, spectacles on the edge of his nose. He looked up as Abby neared.

"May I help you, madam?"

"Yes, I'm looking for some information on the history of the Pulteney family of Bathwick?"

"Yes, history," the gentleman replied. As he climbed off his stool, she followed him to a bookshelf labeled *history*. He walked around the corner, fingering the books. "We have them alphabetically arranged. You may also look in the B's for Bathwick," he suggested. "If you have any other questions, just let me know." He left her to her search and returned to his desk.

Abby ran her fingers along the books until she found a few, then she pulled them out and took them to a table.

"My lady, may I go and look at books?" Betsy asked.

"Yes." Abby smiled. "I'll be right here."

Over the next hour, Abby perused the books as well as newspapers the clerk brought to her. Sir Andrew came from an honorable family. His grandfather had married into wealth, and his wife inherited the Bathwick Estate from her father. Sir Andrew's grandfather commissioned the building of the Pulteney Bridge over the Avon River so they could connect to the town without having to take the ferry. Andrew's father continued the building efforts and helped improve the community of Bath.

Through newspaper articles, she read that Sir Andrew was responsible for getting the new workhouse started in Bathwick. It would be larger and more efficient than the current one she had visited with Miss Stewart and would house another one hundred people in need.

Abby started as the bell tower struck noon. Gathering up the books, she left them on the side table to be put back on the shelves by the clerk.

Outside, the same elegant carriage that she had ridden to Bath in sat by the roadside. A driver stepped down and opened the door. Abby found Aunt Lucy and Mr. Albert seated together inside.

"Did you find what you were looking for, my dear?"

Abby settled into the plush leather seat and leaned back. Luxurious blue velvet curtains covered the windows. "Yes, Aunt Lucy, I did."

CHAPTER FIFTEEN

*I*t didn't take long to reach Sir Andrew's estate, a mere thirty minutes. They crossed the Pulteney Bridge, with its unusual shops on both sides spanning the Avon River. Approaching Sydney Gardens, the carriage swung left onto Beckford Road. Soon they turned onto Sir Andrew's Bathwick land, and the carriage rolled down the long gravel road lined with trees. Abby peered from the window, waiting in anticipation to get a view of the estate.

The house came into view as the trees thinned out. She was pleased with the home. It wasn't as large as her father's but was majestic all the same, built with the same Bath sandstone that many of the other local buildings had used. It comprised three stories of the Greek revival period.

The carriage pulled to a stop at the entrance to the home. Sir Andrew stood, waiting, dressed in the latest fashion. Abby found her heart beating faster at the sight of him. He didn't wait for the footman but opened the door himself. A welcoming smile greeted them.

"Miss Phelips, Mr. Albert, welcome."

Sir Andrew's eyes turned to Abby as he reached out to help her. "Lady Abigale, I look forward to showing you my home."

Abby had no choice but to take his hand. Shivers ran up her arm as she stepped from the carriage, causing her to pull her hand from his as quickly as possible. She moved to the door, speaking to hide her discomfort. "Sir Andrew, I was impressed when your estate came into view from the carriage." Abby looked up, admiring the four Corinthian columns supporting the balcony on the second story.

"Thank you, Lady Abigale. My grandfather was involved with the design."

Turning, she watched Mr. Albert gently help her Aunt Lucy from the carriage. When they caught up, Sir Andrew preceded them through the front door into a grand hallway.

He waited until Abby came alongside him. "I have a lite luncheon prepared for us, and then I thought we could take a tour of the house."

Abby brightened. "I would like that." She looked up; Sir Andrew watched her. His facial features seemed relaxed; gone were the brow lines and the serious expression she had seen so frequently this past month. He looked younger, relaxed in his own surroundings.

They left the hall, opening a door into a morning room where windows stretched across the back. Sir Andrew guided them to the terrace where a table with a white linen tablecloth had been set with pretty Dresden china trimmed in gold and crystal stemware.

A beautiful floral arrangement sat in the center of the table, surrounded by cold sandwiches, pastries, fruit, and a clear pitcher of strawberry lemonade, her favorite. The sight was delightful, Abby thought as Sir Andrew pulled a chair out for her. Mr. Albert assisted her aunt. A pleasant view of the gardens was laid out before them.

"Sir Andrew, you have a fine prospect here," Aunt Lucy commented.

"Yes," Sir Andrew agreed. "My father was passionate about landscaping. He hired Lancelot Brown to design the gardens."

Abby listened intently while Andrew described the history of the grounds. A green stretched out from the house, flanked on both sides by a formal garden. Wooded areas sat away from the home, surrounding a small lake with an interesting feature just barely visible. Abby thought it would be a beautiful place to take her pencils and do a sketch.

"The gardens will be covered with visitors tomorrow, and you may wander and explore at will if you wish." Sir Andrew's eyes warmed as he took in the view. He lifted his glass and took a drink.

"I hope you won't mind if my son joins us for luncheon?" Sir Andrew asked as he put his glass down.

He nodded to the maid standing by the door, who was attired in a crisp white hat and neat grey uniform. The maid quickly returned to the house.

"Not at all," Aunt Lucy replied.

Abby relaxed and popped a few grapes into her mouth, discreetly watching Sir Andrew. His eyes brightened, and she turned to see a small, well-dressed boy being led onto the terrace by an older lady she assumed was the nanny.

His curly hair glistened, and his rosy cheeks and bright smile popped at the sight of his father. "Papa," he exclaimed as he broke free of his nanny and ran toward Sir Andrew.

Sir Andrew scooped him up and sat him on his lap. "William, I would like you to meet Miss Phelips and her niece, Lady Abigale."

"How do you do, Master William," Aunt Lucy replied. "This is my good friend, Mr. Albert. We are pleased to meet you."

"Hello."

Abby was enchanted. "Master William, my brother's name is William."

The young boy looked into her eyes. "I was named after my grandfather," he proudly announced.

Everyone laughed at Master William's pronouncement. He clapped with excitement as everyone gave him their attention. He turned his eyes to his father. "Pretty lady."

Sir Andrew looked up at Abby. "Yes, William, she is

pretty. But I'm afraid she's too old for you," Andrew
chuckled as he put his son in the high chair next to him
where a small place setting had been provided for the
young boy.

Abby felt her cheeks grow warm at the look in Sir
Andrew's gaze. She busied herself with her lunch as the
conversation continued. Abby was awed at the attention
Sir Andrew dealt his son. A warm glow of admiration
filled her.

Andrew watched Lady Abigale blush at his son's
outburst. He hoped that she would like William. It was
important that his next wife be able to accept and love
his son. Although he didn't require love for himself, he
knew the damage of being unloved could cause in a
small child. Hadn't he seen it in the faces of the
workhouse children?

His son behaved himself for the rest of the meal, and
soon, it was time for him to go back to the nanny.
Andrew stood and picked him up. "If you be good for
Nanny, William, you can play with the children
tomorrow at the garden party."

"Party." William happily clapped his hands. He
leaned in, giving his father a big kiss on the cheek, then
turned to Abby and reached out his hands.

She reached over and took him from his father.
Master William beamed. "Pretty lady, come to the

garden party?"

Lady Abigale laughed. "Yes, Master William, I will be at the party."

Andrew was surprised as he watched his son wrap his arms around her neck and give her a tight squeeze before placing a little kiss on her cheek.

The nanny stepped forward, retrieving William from Lady Abigale's arms. He happily waved to his father as she took him into the house.

"I apologize, Lady Abigale, if my son's exuberance embarrassed you," Andrew said.

"Not at all, Sir Andrew." Her eyes followed his son as the nanny took him into the house. "He is a delightful child. You must be so proud of him."

"Yes," Andrew replied, "he brings me great joy."

"You must miss his mother greatly."

Andrew coughed. What could he say? He didn't miss his late wife as much as he should.

"I thought we could take a tour of the house if you are not too tired?" Andrew changed the subject.

"Oh, yes," Lady Abigale replied. "I should love to take a tour now if Aunt Lucy is up to it." She turned concerned eyes on her aunt.

"Yes, dear, I think I can manage it." She chuckled. Standing, Mr. Albert quickly came to her side and helped her to her feet.

Andrew bowed, leading Lady Abigale back into the house, trailed by her aunt and Mr. Albert.

They entered the great hall again while Sir Andrew pointed to the right where the staircase wound up to the next level. "If you look up the stairwell, you'll see to the floors above. As you reach the first landing, the stairs turn along the outer wall and then on the next floor in a spiral pattern. It lets in light from the rear windows as well as contains the staircase on the backside of the home, allowing for more space on each level."

Abby touched the ironwork banister with its intricate pattern. It was unusual from the usually carved wood balustrade found in most country estates.

"The library sits over here," Sir Andrew directed. He walked to the right and opened a panel door, allowing Abby to walk ahead of him. Bookshelves lined two of the walls, and a magnificent fireplace stood at the end. Sir Andrew walked in and leaned on the mantel, watching her while she moved about the room.

Four tall windows flanked the wall opposite the fireplace with neat window seats tucked underneath. Abby fingered the cushions done in jewel tones of green and gold. The room had a masculine feel, yet the lady of the house would feel comfortable as well. She could see herself sitting here, reading a book, or sketching the landscape.

"Do you like the view?"

Abby jumped at the sound of his voice, so near. Her

hand flew to her chest to calm her racing heart. She hadn't known he was so close.

"I didn't mean to startle you." He chuckled as he took a step back.

Abby could still feel the heat of his body. He hadn't moved back enough, for she couldn't move due to the window seat. Taking a breath, she willed her nerves to calm. "I just thought this would be a lovely place to read a book or sketch the prospect. It's the same view from the terrace. What is that building down by the lake?" Sir Andrew leaned over her shoulder as he looked out the window, causing her pulse to pick up speed again.

He straightened up and moved back as Aunt Lucy and Mr. Albert stepped over to admire the view.

"That's the lake cottage. My mother spent time there with her friends, having tea parties while the children swam in the lake," Sir Andrew explained. "I can't remember the last time I have walked down there."

Abby thought she heard wistfulness in his voice but shook the thought from her mind when they turned to leave.

There was a large drawing room at the front of the house where Abby tried to imagine Sir Andrew entertaining guests. His study was pointed out, but they didn't enter. They were shown into a smaller drawing room where a desk sat among the furniture. Abby noticed toys in the corner.

"I like to spend time with William when I'm home. I watch him play and get a few things done. This room is friendlier than my study," Sir Andrew explained, waving his hand towards the toys.

Abby thought of her own father, whom she saw very little of growing up. She liked the idea of a father spending more time with his children.

They returned to the hallway and back down the stairs to the first floor, entering the ballroom, which spanned the whole length of the house. Large windows let in light. French doors opened out onto the portico, supported by the Corinthian pillars she had admired when she first arrived. Abby walked through the doors, admiring the view.

Coming back into the ballroom, Sir Andrew closed the doors behind her. Aunt Lucy and Mr. Albert had settled onto one of the couches at one end of the room. A grand piano, surrounded by chairs, sat at the other end. A small mezzanine above her head supported a small gallery. Portraits lined the walls as Abby stepped over to see them more clearly. Sir Andrew followed, introducing her to his ancestors and telling her a little about each one. The stories were the same that she read in the library.

"My grandfather commissioned this home to be built after he married, and my father improved on the landscape. I admit I have only maintained it. Now that my son is almost three, I will be finishing my term in Parliament and coming home. I won't bid for another term."

"You would do that? Give up your seat in parliament to be home with your son?"

"I would," Sir Andrew answered, his dark, penetrating eyes met hers. "I only wish my father had done the same."

Mine, too, Abby thought to herself.

Abby stepped back, bumping against a small table. She turned, reaching for a vase as it wobbled, almost losing her balance. Sir Andrew reached out and held her tight, steadying her until she gained her footing again. Abby tilted her head up. Sir Andrew's face, only a breath away, caused her to warm again. He studied her mouth before stepping away and releasing her.

"The bedchambers are on the second floor," Sir Andrew told her as they walked towards her aunt. "The housekeeper will show you to your rooms where you can rest before dinner."

The housekeeper directed them to their rooms, where Betsy had laid out an evening gown for dinner. Abby changed into her dressing gown and laid down to rest, but sleep wouldn't come as the events of the day whirled around in her mind.

So many things about Sir Andrew puzzled her. His kindness and love towards his son, the relaxed manner he had here in his home, his willingness to share the history of his life. He hadn't provoked her with a snide comment once, and he had treated her with kindness and respect.

Feelings she didn't understand smoldered just under the surface when he was near. Passion, was that passion he was evoking in her? She had never felt this way around any other gentleman.

She looked at the clock on the mantel. Half an hour had gone by, and still, sleep wouldn't come. Throwing her legs over the side of the bed, she walked over and rang for Betsy.

Her maid came through the door. "Betsy, help me dress, please. I have just enough time to explore that cottage by the lake before dinner."

CHAPTER SIXTEEN

*A*ndrew retired to his room and left his guests to rest before dinner. It had been a pleasant afternoon, but he felt restless while his valet finished his evening attire. Andrew had a couple of hours before dinner and decided to check out the lake. He hadn't been there for years. He retrieved the key from his housekeeper and took a shortcut around the woods.

The lake came into view. The stone cottage stood one hundred yards back. It was Andrew's mother's favorite place, and Andrew remembered all the children playing at their annual garden party.

Just like now, the children liked to play and float their toy boats in the lake. It wasn't large, and only four to five feet deep.

The workers had been busy clearing the brush away and trimming the hedges. Flowers of all colors had been planted around in preparation for the garden party tomorrow. He reached the porch and unlocked the door, sliding the key back in his pocket, and turned the knob. He was surprised nothing had changed. The room was clean of dust. Two high back leather chairs sat facing a floral couch. Windows along the front allowed for a view of the lake.

He relaxed into one of the leather chairs. Closing his eyes, he wrestled with the feelings Lady Abigale caused within him whenever she was near. Touching his breast pocket, he felt paper beneath the fabric. It was his list. He promised himself to give it to Lady Abigale today.

A shadow crossed the window; a mumble of voices could be heard outside. Someone had dared to disturb Andrew's solitude. It was probably the groundsmen. He stood, thinking it would be good to talk with them about the progress for tomorrow's activities.

Andrew rounded the corner of the cottage, surprised to see Lady Abigale swinging back-and-forth gently in the porch swing gazing at the lake, a light shawl about her shoulders. She was dressed for dinner. His heart tightened.

"A peaceful sight, isn't it?" He walked over.

"Yes, it is." She looked up. A smile played about her lips. "I hope you don't mind. I was restless and wanted to explore this feature before dinner. It really is peaceful. I should like to bring pencils down tomorrow and sketch."

"I think we can gather some for you." Sir Andrew

sat down on the swing next to Lady Abigale, leaving space between them. She twirled lavender stems between her fingers, which released a fresh scent. Comfortable silence followed.

He reluctantly pulled the paper from his breast pocket and handed it to her.

"What's this?" She opened the folded sheet.

"I told you I would help you. This is a list of gentlemen of good character. My solicitor assures me these men are solid." He pointed to the paper.

"You had your solicitor look into them?" She gazed into his eyes.

Why did she make him feel giddy, like a young schoolboy? She just had to say the word, and he would do anything she asked.

"That was kind of you." She looked down at the paper and smiled. "I am glad Mr. Dalton has your recommendation. I like him."

His heart dropped. It felt like Abigale had stabbed him. Could he actually be jealous of her attention to Mr. Dalton?

"I have already decided to give up Mr. Woodland and Mr. Tingley. They are young officers. I don't think I'd make a good military wife, for I would not want to sit home alone while my husband went to sea."

Her voice was wistful as she gazed out over the lake. Soft, wispy curls dangled in the breeze.

"I would not leave my wife alone," he found himself saying. She looked up, and their eyes locked.

"You wouldn't?" she whispered.

He found his blood boiling at the thought of her marrying anyone but himself. The idea of Mr. Dalton kissing her was driving him mad. "Yes." He leaned in, and, raising his hand, he skimmed his finger along her chin and down the side of her neck. She stilled, gazing into his eyes. He ran his hand down her arm as he moved closer, watching her tongue wet her lips. She leaned in ever so slightly. His desire was strong. He was ready to take her into his arms when her eyes grew wide. She stood suddenly as her fingers fumbled to fold the paper.

"It must be—time for dinner. We should get back. Aunt Lucy will be worried." Her voice trembled. She stepped away but did not retreat.

He stood, taking a deep breath. "Of course, Lady Abigale, you go ahead, I'll be back shortly."

She nodded and retreated quickly back towards the house.

He took another shuddering breath. Sitting back in the swing, he leaned forward, running his hand along his brow. What had he almost done? He knew not to accost young ladies alone with a kiss, but she was not just any young lady. She had pushed her way into his heart, driving him mad with irritation one minute, and enchanting him the next. He relaxed, stood, and slowly made his way back to the house, thankful there would be a crowd here tomorrow. He would be careful not to be alone with Lady Abigale again. He was fortunate she had the sense to retreat back to the safety of the house.

Lady Abigale deserved to be courted properly. He would speak to her father after the party next week.

Abby's heart raced as she made her way towards the house. She was glad Sir Andrew didn't escort her back. She needed time to regain her composure. She didn't know where she found the strength to stop his kiss, for she knew he intended to embrace her.

She wanted that kiss as much as he did, but she wouldn't let him compromise her just for a ring on her finger. If he loved her, she deserved a courtship and a proper proposal without scandal attached. She was thankful for Aunt Lucy's presence. Now, as she looked at the crumpled paper in her hand, she knew that her heart was Sir Andrew's, for no one else would do.

CHAPTER SEVENTEEN

*A*bby woke up the next morning, deliriously happy. The sun was bright and promised to be a good day for the party. Sir Andrew had been respectful and attentive at dinner the night before, and she entertained the four of them, playing on the grand piano.

Abby slipped out of bed, going to the window. There was a flurry of activity below as workers preparing for the crowds set up tables, chairs and tents.

"My lady, Sir Andrew, sent this package for you." Betsy held a brown bundle tied with string.

Abby took the package and sat down on the bed. Untying the strings, she removed the paper to reveal a wooden lap box made for a lady. Abby unlatched the lock to view sheets of paper for drawing, an assortment of lead and colored pencils, and a small penknife with a golden handle for sharpening. Delighted, she ran her hands across the papers and supplies. She lifted the note that lay on top.

Lady Abigale

I hope these tools will help you draw the prospect you so admired yesterday evening.

Yours, A

How thoughtful. She would use them today to capture the cottage by the lake. The place where she almost received her first kiss.

They all rode in Sir Andrew's carriage for Sunday's services. Master William sat next to his nanny, poking his head around her and watching Abby, a sunny smile on his face. The chapel was already filling when they entered and settled into a pew toward the front. Abby had just seated herself next to her aunt when she felt a small tug from her skirt. William was attempting to climb on her lap. She lifted him up, and he snuggled and relaxed against her, slipping his thumb into his mouth.

"I see you have made a new friend, Abby, dear," Aunt Lucy smiled.

"It seems so." She laughed.

The child's hair, smelling of fresh soap, tickled Abby's nose. Master William's eyes grew heavy as the sermon continued, and he soon fell into a peaceful sleep. Contentment washed over her as she watched the child's slow, steady breathing. He was so easy to love, unlike his father, who had sent feelings of conflict through her ever since they met. She could feel Sir Andrew's eyes upon her, yet she dared not look. Content to enjoy the child, she focused on the sermon.

Master William woke as soon as the service concluded. Wiggling off her lap, he made his way down the aisle, his nanny chasing behind.

The guests had already started gathering as the carriage stopped at the entrance to Sir Andrew's estate. Abby realized she wouldn't be seeing as much of Sir Andrew that day. Master William was running up the steps. "I can see that you are going to be busy, Sir Andrew. It seems your son is eager to get started." Abby gave him a reassuring smile.

"I hope we can spend a little time together throughout the day, it seems my son has attached himself to you." Sir Andrew gazed down at her.

Abby could feel her face warm, and it wasn't because of the weather. "I would like that, Sir Andrew."

"Till later, then. Luncheon is served on the green in back, and servants will be there to help you with anything you need," Sir Andrew informed them.

"We will be fine, Sir Andrew. You go ahead and take care of your other guests," Aunt Lucy said.

Abby watched with a contented heart as Andrew hurried off to do his duty. She planned on spending a relaxing few hours under the shade of the tree while sketching the lake.

"Aunt Lucy, I'm going to run upstairs and retrieve

my pencils. You must take Mr. Albert down to the lake, the one with the little cottage just past the wooded patch. It is very peaceful, and I think it would be a great place to eat our luncheon. I confess I visited there yesterday."

Her aunt nodded. "Mr. Albert, what do you say we take a little walk down by the lake?"

"That would be fine, my dear. Would you like me to get your parasol?"

"I will get it, Mr. Albert, since I'm going upstairs to retrieve my drawing supplies," Abby replied.

"Thank you, dear. Then we will see you out by the lake." Her aunt smiled.

Abby watched Mr. Albert and her aunt walk towards the back terrace. It touched her heart to see him so attentive. They really were a perfect match.

Abby quickly pulled off her bonnet as she entered her room. "Betsy, I want to change into my muslin with the pink cotton underskirt. I think it will be much cooler." She picked a straw bonnet with matching ribbons. "Betsy, will you retrieve a parasol from my aunt's room? I need to take it with me."

"Yes, my lady." Betsy left, quickly returning a few minutes later, just as Abby reached for her drawing supplies.

"Betsy, you look nice. That's a very pretty dress. After we take the parasol to my aunt, you are to enjoy yourself for the rest of the day. I see that you have our things packed. Sir Andrew has arranged a carriage to take us home this evening."

Abby found her aunt under the shade of an old oak, sunlight dappling through the leaves, adding to her aunt's already glowing countenance. Servants had set chairs and tables around the lake. Children played; it was a pleasant scene. Betsy handed the parasol to her aunt before leaving.

"You were right, Abby. This is a very nice place to eat. I see why you wanted to come here," her aunt said.

"Where is Mr. Albert?" Abby slid her drawing set under the table and sat down.

"He has gone over to the refreshment tent to get us some food." Her aunt waved her hand in the direction he'd gone.

"I confess I am famished. There looks to be many delightful things to eat." Abby's hand went to her stomach.

"We cannot have you starve, Lady Abigale; I shall be honored to bring you a plate." The boyishly handsome Mr. Dalton came into view, bowing over her hand.

"Mr. Dalton, do you know what a young lady would like to eat?" Abby enjoyed their playful banter. He reminded her of her brother, William.

"I know what my sister likes. Shall I bring you the same?"

Abby laughed at his safe comeback. "Yes, I think that will do."

"Splendid. I am up for the challenge." Mr. Dalton rubbed his hands together as he headed towards the food table.

Mr. Alfred returned with two plates and set them on the table. "Lady Abigale, may I get you a plate of food?"

"Thank you, Mr. Albert, but Mr. Dalton has gone to gather a plate for me."

"Abby has plenty of gentlemen flying about her, Mr. Albert. I have no doubt she shall be completely taken care of today." Aunt Lucy gave her a pleasant smile.

Yes, Abby thought, she didn't doubt that, but there was only one gentleman she cared to be pampered by, and he would be busy taking care of his guests like an excellent host.

"Here we are, Lady Abigale." Mr. Dalton set two plates of food on the table. "You must tell me how I have done." He sat, taking the chair next to her.

Abby pulled off her gloves and examined the little sandwiches, surrounded by fruit, with two dainty bite-size pastries set on the edge. She picked up a pastry and slid it into her mouth. Footmen had followed with a tray of food, which they set on the table. Another footman appeared with glasses and a pitcher of lemonade.

Abby licked her fingers in a very unladylike fashion. "I think you have brought reinforcements, Mr. Dalton." She giggled.

"Just to be sure I had everything you like. I see that you like dessert first."

"You have found me out, Mr. Dalton. I am partial to sweets." She smiled sweetly, picking up her fork.

After luncheon, Mr. Dalton helped Abby move her chair to a better location so she could draw the cottage. Aunt Lucy and Mr. Albert strolled along the lake's edge. Children scrambled, playing with their boats and squealing while parents watched.

"Lady Abigale, I will leave you now to your drawing, but might I join you for a walk, say, in an hour?"

"Yes, Mr. Dalton, I would like that." She watched as he strolled back towards the gardens. Relaxing, she began drawing the cottage, capturing the children at play by the pond. She set the paper aside and started another drawing of the lake with the grove of trees on the other side.

"You've captured it well." A familiar voice spoke above her. She looked up to see Sir Andrew admiring her drawing of the cottage and pond. She felt that familiar buzz, which permeated her body whenever he was near. Reaching down, she picked up the drawing and handed it to him. He took it and sat down beside her chair, stretching out his legs and leaning his elbow against the grass as he examined it closer.

"I like the way you've captured the children playing by the pond."

"I couldn't have drawn it without your gift. Thank you for the paper and pencils. That was very generous of you."

He shrugged. "I'm glad you have enjoyed them." Sitting up, he looked at her other drawing. "You're very good."

"It is one of the few pursuits that I enjoyed other than playing the pianoforte. I suppose if you like something enough, you put the time and effort into learning the skill. Drawing allowed me to escape the schoolroom and be out in nature," Abby admitted.

Sir Andrew handed back the drawing, looking into her face intently. She couldn't make out what he was thinking but felt the attraction between them, pulling them together. Could this be the passion she'd always sought?

"Lady Abigale, I regret that I haven't been able to spend much time with you today, but I hope I can take you on a walk later and show you the grounds?"

"I would like that." Abby held his gaze.

Sir Andrew reached down and took her bare hand. Their skin touched, and searing heat rippled up her arm. He placed a kiss on the back before letting go. "Until then, Lady Abigale." He turned and strolled towards the house.

Leaning back, she watched him until he was out of sight, a soft smile upon her lips as she gazed out over the lake. Aunt Lucy had been watching, her eyes twinkling with understanding before turning towards Mr. Albert again.

Abby sighed. If this was what it felt like to be in love, then she was . . . in love.

CHAPTER EIGHTEEN

*M*r. Dalton returned a little later than expected, apologizing. "Forgive me, Lady Abigale, it took me a little longer. Are you still up for that walk?"

"I believe so, I have nearly fallen asleep." Abby stood. "Aunt Lucy, Mr. Dalton would like to take me for a walk."

"It is not far, Miss Phelips. There is a little feature I'd like her to see just past the bowling green."

"Then enjoy yourselves. We will go nowhere until you return," Lady Abigale's aunt replied.

Abby took Mr. Dalton's proffered arm, and he led her around the grove of trees, past the formal gardens along the bowling green, and into a small, wooded area. The people began to thin out.

Abby became nervous as they moved into an overgrown path. "Mr. Dalton, if Sir Andrew hadn't told me of your good character, I might be a little nervous right now without a chaperone. I believe we are almost alone."

"Sir Andrew spoke highly of me? I am quite flattered. But I promise to be on my best behavior, Lady Abigale. It is but just a few feet farther."

Mr. Dalton was right. A few more feet and they came upon a quaint little gazebo made in the Greek style with pillars. Abby stepped into the enclosure. Mr. Dalton had cleaned the seats, and a blanket lay across the stone bench, making a place to sit without messing her gown. She sat and gazed out across the lake. She could see the cottage and her aunt strolling with Mr. Albert, yet they were secluded in the private little sanctuary on the other side.

Mr. Dalton turned. Grasping her hand, he knelt before her. Abby froze as she anticipated what he was about to do. No— no, no, she thought.

Sir Andrew did his duty as quickly as he could, anxious to return to Lady Abigale. He could steal away for a short time to show her the grounds before evening set in, but he had always personally said goodbye to each guest. A ritual their family had observed for as long as he could remember.

He hoped that Lady Abigale would be there by his side in the future, helping him in the years ahead. He found her empty chair with her pencils set aside, but no Lady Abigale.

"I was looking for your niece. Do you know where she went?" Sir Andrew asked her aunt.

"Mr. Dalton took her for a walk to see a feature just past the bowling green, I think he said."

Sir Andrew looked up. A feature by the bowling green. He peered across the lake. He could just barely see the gazebo nestled in the wooded area.

"Thank you, Miss Phelips." Sir Andrew turned and quickly walked towards the gazebo.

His stomach flipped, knots forming as he increased his pace. He entered the path in the wooded area and stopped as they came into view. Lady Abigale sat on the bench. Mr. Dalton reached for her hand and knelt by her side.

"Lady Abigale, you must know I'm crazy about you. Will you be my wife?"

Abigale pulled her hand from Mr. Dalton's. "Benjamin, you know I adore you." She reached her trembling hand out, brushing a stray lock on his forehead.

Andrew turned, retreating quietly, not willing to disturb the intimate scene. His heart turned cold. He was too late. Fires of jealousy burned within him as he tried to shut out the scene. She called him Benjamin. Had their relationship advanced faster than he realized? Hadn't she told him she liked Mr. Dalton very much?

Andrew made it to the house without talking to

anyone and shut himself in his study, locking the door behind him. He poured himself a glass of liquor, not caring which one. Andrew twirled the glass under his nose. What was he doing? Andrew looked at the liquid then threw the glass across the room into the fireplace, shattering the glass as it hit the bricks. He wasn't a drinking man, and nobody was going to make him into one, not even Abigale, who had made her way into his heart, only to shatter it.

Abby's heart constricted as she looked into Mr. Dalton's pleading eyes, gently pulling her trembling hand from his. "Benjamin, you know that I adore you." She reached towards him, pushing a lock of hair off of his forehead. Just as she would her brother. There was no passion in his touch, no sizzle, or anticipation. "I cannot, for I've given my heart to another." She smiled to soften the blow.

He relaxed, drawing his hands away, he sat beside her. "It's Sir Andrew, isn't it?"

She blushed, nodding her head.

"If I were Sir Andrew sitting here, your answer would've been different, wouldn't it?"

She nodded her head again, afraid to say it out loud.

"Well." Mr. Dalton sighed. "I should be jealous, but I'm not. That must mean something, right?"

"I'm glad I have not broken your heart, Mr. Dalton, but I hope that we can be friends."

"Friends? Yes, Abby, I would like that. Can I call you, Abby?"

"Of course, if I can call you Benjamin." She giggled as the tension defused between them.

Mr. Dalton stood and offered Abby his hand. "I better return you to your aunt. I would hate to compromise you." He smiled.

The walk back to the lake was relaxing. Abby's heart warmed from seeing her aunt sitting under a tree with Mr. Albert, her pencils undisturbed. She sat down and took them out, and Benjamin joined them.

"Did Sir Andrew find you, Abby?" her aunt asked.

"Sir Andrew? Was he looking for me?"

"Yes, dear, but I expect he'll be back if he didn't find you."

Her heart sunk. The sound of laughing children caught her attention. Master William was playing with a toy boat happily while his nanny sat, talking with the other women. Older boys pushed their boats around the pond.

Abby pulled out her pencils and began to sketch Master William. His curly hair had fallen over his brow, and his rosy cheeks stood out in the heat of the afternoon. She quickly drew, trying to catch the moment before the child moved away. A gift for Sir Andrew, to thank him for a delightful weekend, she thought.

She glanced up from her sketch to see Master

William walking towards the edge of the pond, his arm outstretched with his boat, ready to drop it in the water. Abby stood and raced towards the lake, fearing that he might fall in. Master William did, headfirst, into the water as his boat moved away on the waves the boy had created. Abby jumped without thinking, scooping the child up as he sputtered, crying out, clinging to her neck. She held him tight for a few minutes as her pulse slowed. He was safe. She turned to see his boat bobbing away on the ripples.

"Boat, boat," Master William cried.

CHAPTER NINETEEN

*A*ndrew sat in the nearest chair, bent over, his hands cradling his head as his son's sharp cry brought him to attention. The screams came from a distance, down by the lake. He stood, quickly walking to the window. Crowds were moving towards the lake. His son's loud cry could still be heard.

Andrew ran outside, making it to the hill as the lake came into view. He could see Abigale waist-deep in the lake, his son clinging to her neck while she walked towards the edge. She handed William to his nanny, dripping from head to toe. Abigale turned towards the lake and reached for William's toy boat. An older lad swam over, and, grabbing the boat, he handed it to Abigale. She turned to make her way back to the lake's edge.

"Master William, see?" Lady Abigale waved the

boat toward Master William. "Abby has saved your boat."

Mr. Dalton reached for the boat and took it from Abby's hands, handing it to his son, William. The child quieted down while the nanny turned and started toward the house.

Andrew tried to wrap his mind around the scene before him. His son was safe now, but somehow, he'd fallen into the lake where Abby had rescued him. Andrew managed to move forward. Abigale climbed out of the lake. Wet from the waist down, her thin dress clung to her shapely silhouette for all to see.

Mr. Dalton turned his back as her aunt quickly ran to her aid, wrapping her shawl around her. But it was too late. The picture was emblazoned upon his mind, etched in his memory to torture him forever of the woman he could not have.

The crowds thinned out as the participants moved towards the house. His nanny approached; William had started to cry again, whining for Abby.

"I'm sorry, sir, I should have watched him better," his nanny said.

Andrew reached for his son and took him from her arms. The boy clung to his neck, laying his head on his shoulder, and quieting as he slipped his thumb into his mouth for comfort. He watched Abigale making her way forward with her aunt beside her, Mr. Dalton, on the other. His coat around her shoulders further shielded her from embarrassment, and his arm wrapped around her waist for support. They drew alongside him.

"Lady Abigale, do I have you to thank for rescuing my son from the lake?" Sir Andrew asked, his voice thick and husky.

"I wouldn't call it a rescue." She laughed. "But yes, Master William tumbled over into the water while trying to put his boat into the pond."

"Boat, Abby, boat," Master William cried, raising his head from his father's shoulder.

"Yes, William, Nanny has your boat," Abby said.

Nanny stepped forward, showing the child his boat as he waved his wet thumb, reaching for it. The nanny placed it into his grip, and he squeezed the boat tight as he laid his head back on his father's shoulder.

"Is there anything I can do for you, Lady Abigale?" Andrew asked, his voice tight.

"No, Sir Andrew. I'm just a little wet. I should be fine after a change. Take care of your son, and we will talk later." She smiled up at him. No sign of distress touched her face.

Andrew quickly turned and retreated toward the house, gripping his son tightly. His son whimpered, "Abby, I want Abby." He cried into his father's shoulder.

Andrew tightened his grip. "I know, son. I do too, but it's too late. We can't have her," he whispered.

∽

Abby watched as Sir Andrew hurried his son into the house, her heart softening with every step. When she reached the terrace, she reassured Mr. Dalton that her Aunt Lucy could take care of her.

"It was a delightful day, Abby. I shall call before I head back to Bristol." He bowed.

"Thank you, Benjamin." She gave him a warm smile and squeezed his hand before turning and making her way back to her room.

Betsy arrived shortly after hearing about the ruckus. "Oh, my lady, it's true, then, you jumped into the lake." She brought Abby's drawing set and her sketches and laid them on the dresser.

"Yes, Betsy, I jumped into the lake. What else would a proper lady do to save a drowning child?" She laughed.

"Betsy, I know you've packed all of my things, but could you find a dry dress for me to drive home in tonight?"

"Yes, my lady." She quickly left the room, leaving Abby standing with her aunt.

"This day didn't end quite as I planned." Abby sighed. She feared she'd missed an opportunity to talk with Sir Andrew, as he would be busy with his son.

"Never mind, dear, it was a lovely weekend. You were brave to jump in the lake like that. You never were one to worry about your clothes or how you looked." Her aunt chuckled. "No matter how hard I tried."

Her maid had convinced footmen to remove a bag

from the carriage to retrieve a dry dress from her luggage. Dressed in dry clothes, Abby felt much better. It was time for them to leave, but Sir Andrew did not make an appearance as she waited in the hall. She left the sketch of Master William on the side table in the hallway.

She would have liked to have seen him before she left but understood his need for staying with his son. The ride back to Mrs. Notley's home was uneventful. It had been a glorious weekend. She looked forward to seeing Sir Andrew the following week.

Andrew woke the next morning having had a restless night of sleep, visions of Abby standing by the lake, her dress clinging to her shapely figure, driving him mad. When had he started thinking of her as Abby and not Lady Abigale?

She had enchanted his son, who kept asking for her throughout the evening. William had been bathed and quickly settled back into his regular routine. Andrew read him a story before tucking him in for the night. He'd fallen asleep immediately. If only his own night had been as peaceful.

He would get back to his projects and work just as he had before Abigale came into his life. He would get through this.

Andrew was passing through the hall on his way to

the study when a piece of parchment caught his eye. Coming closer, he stared down into the face of his son, William, playing with his boat beside the lake. She had captured his playfulness and innocence of youth. He folded it reverently and slid it into his waistcoat pocket.

CHAPTER TWENTY

*A*bby's week continued pretty much as before. She visited the workhouse with Miss Underwood, who had gathered clothing for the children through her women's society. It was good to see the children again, she thought as she brought them more candy. She borrowed a few novels from the lending library and enjoyed the ice shop and walks through the park, but the parties weren't as bright as they had been before. She missed Isabella and Benjamin, but especially Sir Andrew.

Pacing the drawing room, Abby felt restless. "Aunt Lucy, if it weren't improper, I would dare write Sir Andrew. I was sure he felt something toward me. I must have done something to give him a dislike of me."

Her aunt laid down her stitching, giving Abby a sympathetic look. "I know you can be impulsive, Abby, but I have seen nothing in your actions to cause offense." She looked at Mr. Albert. "I hesitate to admit that we saw interest as well. We are surprised he hasn't asked for your hand by now."

Abby deflated and sat next to her aunt. "I thought so as well, but I don't know anymore."

"Why don't I make a trip over and visit Sir Andrew myself?" Mr. Albert offered.

"Really? You would do that for me?" Abby brightened.

"Lionel, that would be wonderful," her aunt exclaimed.

"Yes, dear, I hope that I can bring you the good news you seek and put both your minds at ease." Mr. Albert looked at her aunt lovingly before turning a smile on Abby.

Abby relaxed. If Mr. Albert should bring news that Sir Andrew had been put off by her, then she would try to be happy as she was before, Abby tried to convince herself.

Abby paced the drawing room the next day as her aunt watched her back-and-forth movements.

"Abby, dear, you're as bad as William was when he was worried about Eliza. Pacing will not bring the answer any sooner. Lionel will be here when he can."

Abby stopped and sat next to her aunt. "You and Mr. Albert have become very close. I have noticed he is very tender towards you."

Her aunt blushed. Abby could not believe the

happiness in her countenance. She was like a young schoolgirl. Finally, to have found love.

"I hesitate to tell you our news, Abby, with you being so distressed over Sir Andrew."

"Aunt Lucy, I would not wish to rain on your happiness. I shall be fine whatever the outcome."

Her aunt looked into her face as if to gauge the truth of Abby's words. "Lionel has asked for my hand, and I have accepted."

Abby's eyes began to pool as she reached for her aunt and embraced her in a tight hug. "I am so happy to see that you have found someone." Abby pulled away. "You deserve some happiness in your life."

Her aunt patted her hand and gave it a squeeze. "Abby, I have been happy. You have brought more joy to my life than I can say."

A tear slipped from Abby's eye, and she wiped it with the back of her hand.

"Abby, it was my choice not to marry. I can tell you now because I think you're old enough, and it might help you in some way."

Abby nodded and relaxed next to her aunt.

"I had many gentlemen pursue me when I was young, and then I gave my heart to one, and we were to be married. Your father, older and wiser than me, checked into his character. His solicitor found that he was a bounder, a dishonorable man who only wanted my fortune. He had a wife in another town. It was hard to hear, but fortunately, your father found him out before we were married." Her aunt gave her a sad smile.

"I was heartbroken, of course, and vowed not to marry. It was easier. Until Mr. Albert, my heart never healed."

"Mr. Albert healed your heart?"

Her aunt laughed. "Yes, he has, but then so have you, Abby. I have loved being a part of your life."

The door opened, and Mr. Albert walked in, his eyes brightened at the scene before him. "You have told her?"

"Yes, Lionel, I have told her."

Abby came forward, giving Mr. Albert a hug and a kiss on both cheeks. "I'm so happy for you both."

Mr. Albert walked over and took her aunt's hand. "Do you have news, Lionel?" her aunt asked.

He nodded, looking up. "I'm afraid when I reached Sir Andrew's home, I was told that he had left for London."

"London! When?" Abby sat down in the nearest chair, trying to take the news in. Why would he go to London? "Did they say when he would return?"

"No, the butler said they didn't expect him home for quite some time." Mr. Albert gave her a sympathetic look. "I wish it could have been better news."

Shocked, Abby stood, her eyes pooling with water again as she wiped a tear from her cheek. No wonder he hadn't called. How soon had he left for London? Had it been right after the party?

"Aunt Lucy, I think I'm ready to go home." Abby's shoulders slumped.

"Yes, dear, we understand." Her aunt looked into her intended's eye. "We will make the arrangements."

Abby walked to her room. She would have Betsy start packing. There was nothing left for her here. Suddenly she missed her family.

Sir Andrew, determined to get his life back to normal, visited the workhouse to check how the plans were progressing for the new workhouse at Bathwick. He was informed of Miss Underwood's and Lady Abigale's donations of clothes and candy for the children.

He'd also observed her strolling through the park several times with Mr. Dalton this past week. He was perplexed as to why she hadn't returned home to get ready for her wedding. By the second week, he'd had enough. The tension was building, and he was having a hard time resisting the urge to visit her. Fearful he might say something he would regret, he returned to London, to keep a safe distance.

But London was hot, dirty, and sweltering, not the best combination for Andrew's mood. Unhappy that he was run from his country home, he tried to make the best of it. It had been over a fortnight, and he'd been scouring the papers every day for an announcement of Lady Abigale's engagement to Mr. Dalton. But they were silent. He laid the paper on the table in frustration.

Lifting his cup, he took a drink of his coffee. It had grown cold. He glanced across the room over the rim of his cup. There sat Sir George. Strange that he would be in the club at this late date. He would have thought he'd be home in the country with his daughter. Setting the cup down, he moved across the room to join him.

"Sir George." Andrew offered his hand as he came near.

Sir George stood, grasping his outstretched hand and giving Andrew's a firm shake. "Sir Andrew, what are you doing in London?"

"Just some business before I return to the country. I could ask you the same, Sir George. I thought you would be in the country now with your daughter."

"I had a few things to finish, but I should be leaving this week," Sir George replied.

"Congratulations on the betrothal. You must be pleased."

"Oh, yes." Sir George chuckled. "I had given up on the old girl, but she finally came through. My daughter wrote and is thrilled. Smitten, she said. I think they will be very happy together."

Andrew's heart tightened at the news. Jealousy rose again as he tried to tamp it down. It was an uncomfortable feeling that made him shift in his chair.

"My sister wrote that you took good care of my Abby. She said you made sure she was properly chaperoned. Thank you for that, Sir Andrew. I owe you a great favor, as I know it was a great inconvenience to you. I would like you to come out to the wedding. It's at the end of the week. You may stay at our home. I know my sister would be delighted to see you again. It will get you out of this London heat."

Sir Andrew was tempted, but he didn't think he could watch Lady Abigale marry Mr. Dalton. He might do something that would embarrass himself.

"I thank you for the offer, Sir George. I will have to check my schedule."

"Fine, I will send you directions if you decide you can make it."

Andrew wanted to leave but didn't want to be rude. "Give my best to the couple. I know Mr. Dalton to be of fine character."

Sir George's brows wrinkled. "Mr. Dalton? I don't think I know him."

Andrew settled back in his chair, confused. "Mr. Benjamin Dalton, the groom?"

"My sister is marrying Mr. Albert, Mr. Lionel Albert."

"Your sister—" Andrew felt his head in a fog. "I thought Lady Abigale was marrying Mr. Dalton?"

"Was that his name?" Sir George asked. "Lucy told me Abby had received a proposal, but she turned him down, claiming she'd given her heart to someone else. But that gentleman never came up to scratch. She was so disappointed they came home. Abby swears she'll never marry, but I'm sure she'll change her mind. Abby is a bright girl with a cheery attitude. Nothing gets her down for long."

Sir Andrew lost his train of thought as his body vibrated.

Abby said no. She'd given her heart to someone else. Hope began to bubble inside him. "Sir George, I believe I shall make room in my schedule and accept your invitation to attend Miss Phelips' wedding."

"Good, good." Sir George grinned. He waved his hand, getting the attention of an assistant. "Would you bring me some paper and ink?"

The paper was soon procured, and Sir George wrote the address, date, and time of his sister's wedding before handing it to Andrew. "My sister will be pleased." Sir George beamed.

Andrew floated out of the club; a weight had been lifted, and the world was sunny again.

Abby drifted around the house in a daze. She was surrounded by happy couples, which made her heart heavier. Even the sight of her nephew didn't cheer her up. It only reminded her of Master William. Her father had returned a few days before, cheering her a little. She sat in the drawing room with her family, helping her aunt stitch lace onto her veil. Her dress was simple, and the veil only came to her shoulders, but it would suit her. Eliza's father, the vicar, would perform the ceremony with the family and a few close friends attending.

Her father sat in a comfortable chair. They had just finished breakfast, and he was going over the posts for the day. Cracking the seal, he opened a letter.

"Lucy, you will be happy to hear Sir Andrew will be arriving tomorrow. I've invited him to attend the wedding. I didn't think you would mind as you wrote such good things about him."

"Sir Andrew?" Abby dropped her aunt's veil. Her heart picked up speed as the air left the room. Her head swayed as she struggled to stay upright. Her aunt reached over and took her hand, grounding her to reality. "Sir Andrew? That's wonderful news, George. When did you speak to him?"

"I saw him in the club earlier this week in London. Funny thing, Abby, he thought you were marrying Mr. Dalton. Is that the name of the gentleman you refused?"

"Yes, Father." Abby found her voice. The room started to come back into focus. This was silly. She never fainted. She could do this. She could see Andrew again. Her aunt let go of her hand, watching to make sure she was steady. "Well, this is good news, isn't it, Abby?" Her aunt smiled. "We should be glad to see Sir Andrew again."

Abby smiled while nodding her head, trying to contain her tears, which she felt were ready to fall at any moment. *Sir Andrew thought I was engaged to Benjamin.* No wonder he had avoided her.

Eliza had risen to come to her aid. "Abby, would you help me with something?"

Abby's sister-in-law guided her out of the room, wrapping her arm around her waist, and led her into a private sitting room where they could talk. Eliza handed her a handkerchief while Abby sat in a comfortable chair surrounded by greens and golds. This room had always made her feel calm.

Eliza sat by her side. "You never told me that Isabella's brother Benjamin had asked you to marry him." Her nose scrunched.

"I didn't see the point. I said no." Abby blew her nose.

Eliza shook her head. "But *Benjamin Dalton.* I never figured him to ask someone to marry him."

Eliza had married her brother William a few years ago. They were all three friends growing up. Eliza's father was the vicar, and she had gone to Bristol, where her aunt, Mrs. Notley, was to sponsor her for a Season in Bath. Fortunately for William, they married before she had her Season. They had not been impressed with Benjamin Dalton.

"He was different than you described him. He treated Isabella with respect, and we became friends."

"I am glad if he has changed. Now – what is this about Sir Andrew? You must tell me everything." Eliza sat back, making herself comfortable.

Abby giggled as she dried her tears and told of her adventures, leaving nothing out. Including her trick to get Sir Andrew to bring her to Bath, escaping another day of riding with Mrs. Packett's daughters.

They laughed until the tears rolled before sobering. "Abby, that was a perilous thing for you to do. You're very fortunate that Sir Andrew was honorable, and a friend of your father's."

Abby ducked her head. "I know. It seems Sir Andrew has tamed some wildness in me. I do not desire to run about willy-nilly anymore." Abby sighed.

"Can it be that Lady Abigale is growing up?" Eliza teased.

Abby's lips turned up, showing her bright smile before they dropped again. "I don't think I can face Sir Andrew yet. Why don't we make a trip to Bowood House and visit Susan tomorrow morning?"

Eliza nodded. "I think that's a lovely idea."

CHAPTER TWENTY-ONE

*A*ndrew arrived at Montacute, home of Sir George, just before noon the day before the wedding. The roads were dry, allowing him to make excellent time with his team of four. The estate was vast, and it took a while to reach the main house. When the estate came into view, his breath hitched at the size, for it dwarfed his home in Bathwick. Would Lady Abigale be satisfied living at Bathwick after being raised here? He shook the thought away. He would not doubt himself.

Handing the reins to the groom, he descended from his curricle. His man, Baley, directed the unloading of his luggage. He didn't know how long he would be here, but he vowed not to leave until Lady Abigale consented to be his wife.

Before he reached the door, Sir George appeared

with open arms. "I am glad you've made it safely, Sir Andrew. Come, I want you to meet my son."

The family was gathered on the back terrace. "My son, William." A young man stepped forward, his coloring similar to Abigale's.

"I believe we've met before in London, but it has been a while, Sir Andrew." William shook his hand.

"My sister, Miss Lucy Phelips, and her intended, Mr. Albert, whom you already know."

"Sir Andrew." Miss Phelips came forward. "I was pleased to hear you were coming to the wedding. George tells us there was a little mix-up, but I'm glad it was straightened out. We missed you in Bath." She gave him a pointed look.

It appeared Sir George had been talking, Andrew thought. He didn't see Lady Abigale as he quickly scanned the room.

Mr. Albert stepped forward, offering his hand and wrapping his other one around his intended. You would have thought they were twenty years younger by the way they looked at each other. "We are glad to have you, Sir Andrew."

"Thank you, Mr. Albert." Andrew nodded.

William stepped forward. "Sir Andrew, do you ride?"

"I do, but it has been a while."

"I thought we would take a ride over the estate to give you a tour of the place, but let's get you fed first. My wife and sister have ridden over to Lady Susan's for the morning. They should be back later, which will give us time."

Sir Andrew was disappointed at not seeing Lady Abigale but looked forward to riding. True to William's word, he was fed well then shown to his room where his man had already unpacked.

"I'm going riding, Baley."

"Yes, my lord." He quickly pulled his riding clothes from the wardrobe.

In no time, Andrew was following William to the stables. He was impressed by the fact that the horseflesh was housed in two large buildings.

"We keep the mares over in the other building," William explained. "Our stallions are here."

He followed William into the stable. Stalls lined both sides, with a tack room towards the end and hay in storage. "You have excellent stock." Andrew admired a black stallion, daring to touch his nose while he reared his head up and down. A groom had two beauties already saddled.

Andrew followed William out into the road, taking it slowly until he got the measure of his mount. He was fine horseflesh. Soon they were galloping, the air rushing past, relieving the tension Andrew had been feeling for the past few weeks. William stopped on the crest of a hill where they could see over the countryside. A small village set off to the right, and tenant farms dotted the landscape.

William pointed to a large estate in the distance.

"That is Bowood House, Lord Malmesbury's land, which borders ours."

Andrew breathed in the air. It was a welcoming contrast to London's oppressive heat.

"My father tells us you thought my sister was engaged to Benjamin Dalton?" William shook his head.

"You find that hard to believe?"

"The Benjamin Dalton I knew, yes." William continued to shake his head. "I met him a few years ago while I was courting my wife Eliza in Bristol. I thought he was arrogant and treated his sister abominably."

Andrew thought about the young man he'd seen in Bath. This didn't fit the description of the Mr. Dalton he knew, but he didn't know him very well prior to Lady Abigale coming to town.

"The Mr. Dalton I've known this past summer is very amiable and treats his sister with respect. He's developed a fondness for your sister."

"Yes, I can believe it. My sister is very likable, but I am glad to hear Benjamin has improved." William turned to study him. "Sir Andrew, are you going to ask my sister to marry you?"

Andrew was caught off guard with the blunt question. "I . . . Don't know . . . Why would you ask me that? Has your father said something?"

"No, not in so many words, but I have eyes. You show up for my aunt's wedding after finding out my sister is not spoken for. When my father mentioned that you were arriving today, I saw my sister's reaction,"

William explained. "Abby has not been herself since she returned from Bath, then when your name was mentioned and that you were coming, she brightened up again."

Andrew took courage that he would be well received.

"Do you love my sister?"

Andrew laughed at William's bluntness. "I see you are as open as your sister. Yes, I do. I do love your sister, and she has captured my son's heart as well." Andrew surprised himself with the admission.

"You have a son, then."

"Yes, he will be three this year. He has taken a liking to your sister, and I believe she likes him as well." Andrew thought of the drawing he had tucked away in his pocket.

"Come," William spurred his mount forward, "I believe I see the ladies."

Andrew followed as they galloped towards a copse of trees where he could see three ladies on horseback. As they neared, the three riders turned and moved to greet them. A handsome brunette came alongside William. "Sir Andrew, I'd like to introduce my wife, Lady Eliza, and our friend and neighbor, Lady Susan, the Countess of Malmesbury."

"Lady Susan, Lady Eliza," Andrew tipped his hat, "I am glad to meet friends of Lady Abigale's." His eyes shifted to Abigale, who had moved her mount beside him. A small smile played about her lips, and golden wisps had worked their way from their pins, softly blowing across her cheeks. Andrew swallowed. She was so beautiful. Her friends had moved away, strolling, talking among themselves, and occasionally looking over their shoulders as they gave them some distance.

"Andrew, why have you waited so long to come and visit me?" she asked. Her lip trembled with a little pout. She had used his Christian name. All he wanted to do was wrap her in his arms and kiss that pout away. He reached his hand over but drew back, looking towards her friends.

She noticed his movement and withdrawal. Slapping her reins, she turned her mount, moving towards a wooded area. He watched her friends slowly disappear in the distance before following her. She led them to a wooded area by a brook before she dismounted. Tying the reins to a tree, she grabbed a twig and snapped it off as she walked towards the water. He followed, dismounting and leaving his horse alongside hers, and came to stand beside her. She snapped the twig between her fingers.

"Why would you think I was engaged to Benjamin?" Abigale asked.

"Benjamin?" She just used Mr. Dalton's Christian name.

"We are friends, that is all."

"You said you really liked him," Andrew confessed, feeling uncomfortable with where this conversation was leading.

"You saw us, didn't you?" she whispered. "In the gazebo by the lake? But you didn't stay to hear it all, or else you wouldn't have assumed what you did and left me."

Andrew moved closer, and, reaching over, he took her arms, drawing her toward him. "Your father said you have given your heart to someone else." His fingers tightened. "Who have you given your heart to, Abigale?" he whispered, sliding his hands down her arms and wrapping them around her waist. He tightened his grip as his heart raced. He felt her warmth, determined she would not escape him this time.

She reached up to lay her hand along his cheek. "Are you so blind that you cannot see? I have given it to you, Andrew." She smiled.

He almost swore he heard church bells ringing as the world brightened around him. Holding her tighter, he brought his head down, brushing his lips against hers. As her breath caught and stilled, he deepened the kiss. Her arms entwined around his neck, and she pulled him closer. It was a long time before they came up for air. Her eyes glistening, he guided her towards their mounts.

"Now that I have thoroughly compromised you, you shall not escape. I shall speak to your father when we return."

She reached for his lapels, pulling him closer. "Do we have to return now?" Her eyes gleamed mischievously. "I could use another kiss."

"You little minx." He laughed as he wrapped her in his arms and obliged her with another kiss, and another, and another . . . As they explored each other further.

"Yes," she finally replied as they pulled away, "but I am *your* little minx."

As she ran her hand over his waistcoat, a crackle of paper sounded beneath. She watched him reach in and pull out her drawing. Andrew handed it to her. She unfolded the paper to see Master William's likeness staring back. "How is he doing?"

"He's healthy, thanks to you, but he cries for his Abby. I thought we both had lost you." Andrew reached down. Taking her fingers, he brought them to his lips. She moved closer, and her other arm wrapped around him, pulling him closer. He nuzzled her neck while breathing her in. "You will never lose me," she whispered.

Abby paced before the door of her father's study. It was nervous energy more than anything, for surely her father would be pleased to welcome Andrew into their family. Abby wondered that his kiss could be so delightful as she remembered the passion he evoked in her, still vibrating with the feelings, as her boots tapped along the marble tile. A footman strode by the door, and she lifted her hand, waving at him as she continued to pace. A distant clock struck four. It would soon be time for dinner, she thought, looking at the door once more willing it to open.

Eliza approached, a tenderness in her eyes. She wrapped her arm around Abby's waist and steered her to a bench in the hall. Abby let herself be guided and sat next to Eliza.

"You know how your father is when he gets started on a topic," Eliza reassured her.

"Yes, but he is not in Parliament, giving a speech and trying to get members to vote," Abby pouted.

Abby stood quickly when she heard the door open. Her father laughed as she rushed towards him. "Your intended awaits you, but remember, dinner will be served shortly." Sir George left them with the door open.

"Father said yes?" Abby moved forward, stopping in front of Andrew.

"Yes, my dear Abigale." He reached and took her hands. "I am afraid you are stuck with me." Leaning down, he kissed the tip of her nose.

She liked the sound of her name on his tongue as she moved closer, his musky scent from their afternoon ride making her delirious.

"We just have time to change for your aunt's wedding dinner," Andrew said, guiding her out of her father's study and handing her to Eliza, who waited in the hall.

"We shall talk about our plans after your aunt's wedding. I'll send a note to my parish to have the banns read this Sunday," he promised, giving her one last kiss before she left for her room.

A morning drizzle turned to a downpour. The ceremony ended with sunbeams filtering through the clouds as the happy couple emerged from the chapel and made their way to the wedding carriage.

"I can't believe Aunt Lucy and Mr. Albert are going to be gone for a year." Abby sighed as she watched their carriage disappear down the lane.

Andrew tightened his grip and gave her a reassuring hug as he brought her closer. "I hope you will keep yourself busy planning for our wedding next month."

"Oh, she will," Eliza and Susan said in unison, and the three friends dissolved into laughter.

"Abby, you know that a thorough tour of the continent takes at least a year," her brother William informed her.

"I know William, and Aunt Lucy deserves a life of her own now that we are both grown. I'm just thankful she found Mr. Albert."

Andrew brought her closer, giving her a comforting squeeze. "You shall be so busy enjoying our wedding trip to the Americas, by the time we return home Aunt Lucy will be here and settled."

Abby's eyes grew wide. "The Americas," she whispered.

"Yes, I have business there, and you don't think I would leave my family behind, not for a whole year."

"You know I lost a wager with my sister, because of you, Andrew." William slapped Andrew on the back.

Abby looked over to William and giggled, as Andrew gave her a wink. Warm feelings settled within her.

"Glad I could help old chap," Andrew teased.

"I think you'll fit into the family just fine." William guided Eliza towards their carriage while James and Susan followed.

Abby looked into Andrew's face, a warm smile spreading across her lips. Yes, Abby thought, he will, Andrew will fit in perfectly.

Authors Notes

Our hero Sir Andrew is based on Sir William Pulteney, 5th Baronet. William Johnstone until 1767, was a Scottish advocate, landowner, and politician who sat in the House of Commons. He was reputedly the wealthiest man in Great Britain by his marriage to heiress Frances Pulteney on 10 November 1760. He invested in lands in North America, and in developments in Great Britain, including the Pulteney Bridge.

The English Poor laws required workhouses to be built in each parish and the administration of the poor and indigent was handled by poor law unions. The poor laws of England are very extensive, and a thorough study can be found at workhouses.org.uk

References
    https://en.wikipedia.org/wiki/Sir_William_Pulteney,_5th_Baronet#Early_life
    http://www.workhouses.org.uk/

ABOUT THE AUTHOR

As Karen Lynne, I write sweet historical romances, regency period being my favorite. Encouraged by my daughter a clean contemporary romance author, to write my own stories, I decided to write my first series. I love history and have been reading hundreds of romances since high school. Timeless authors where the hero and heroine are virtuous with sweet happy endings.

When I am not writing, I enjoy time with my sweetheart, my children and grandchildren and long lunches with my two reading buddies. You know who you are.

Gardening vegetables and fruits in my garden and living in our 1863 stone cottage set in the Rocky Mountains. Life if good!

*I*sabella had just returned from Bath as she tiptoed into her Bristol home hoping to avoid her mother at least for a while. She stopped in the hall as she heard footsteps, relieved as Mildred came around the corner.

"Miss Isabella, you're home." Mildred gave her a comforting smile, wiping her hands on a towel. "Do not worry, your mother is not home yet. She went to her ladies' auxiliary meeting and will not be back until this afternoon."

Isabella dropped her hand from her chest in relief. She turned to go up the stairs, while Mildred followed.

"Thank heavens for small blessings," Isabella said. "I need just a little rest from my journey before my mother starts making demands."

"You had a good time then," Mildred asked.

"Oh, yes." Isabella twirled, landing on her bed.

"Lady Abigale was such fun. Things were just getting exciting when mother sent a message to come home."

"I am pleased. I'll bring you some warm water so you can freshen up." Mildred left Isabella to think about her trip; it had been glorious.

It was the first time seeing her friend Abigale; they had been writing for several years. Eliza, Mrs. Notley's niece, had introduced them through letters and they'd been writing ever since. Isabella had been invited to Bath with Mrs. Notley and her niece Joanne, Eliza's younger sister. The Notley's were prominent in the community and respected by both her parents, who allowed Mrs. Notley to escort Isabella to parties and other functions. Mrs. Notley was the only one her mother trusted to escort Isabella beside herself. Mrs. Notley had been allowing Isabella to correspond with her friend through her household. Otherwise, Isabella was sure her mother would read her letters.

Isabella jumped from the bed and rifled through her reticule, searching for the bag given to her by Abigale. It was there as she pulled it out, opening the drawstrings. She emptied the coins upon her bed, counting each one. A note contained the address of Fyne Court, a sanctuary where Isabella could go if need be. But would she? It would take a lot of courage to defy her parents, especially her mother.

Isabella looked around the room, clutching the pouch to her chest. If her mother found this, she would take it. Lifting the feather mattress, she slid it deep underneath. Only Mildred changed the beds so it would be safe for now. Isabella had committed the address to memory just in case. She hated that she was so distrustful, but until Isabella had met Lady Eliza and Lady Abigale, she'd had no friends; her mother made sure of that.

At four and twenty, she was practically a spinster. Whenever she met someone she genuinely liked, her mother interfered. It was easier to obey than suffer the consequences. Her father was no better as he spent most of his time at work.

Isabella went to the mirror and sat, removing her bonnet. Turning her head from side to side, she examined her reflection as her shiny blond curls bounced back and forth. As far as Isabella could tell, an ordinary face stared back at her. Gentlemen had told her she was beautiful but she thought they were just polite, for her mother continually let her know that she was unattractive. Even her brother Benjamin ignored her. Except for this summer when Lady Abigale, Abby, Isabella called her, came for a visit to Bath. Benjamin had suddenly taken an interest in her. She suspected it was Abby he was interested in for her friend had the same blond hair and blue eyes but was stunning, at least Isabella thought so and so did her brother.

They had been invited to a garden party at Sir Andrew's estate. Just when things were getting exciting, her mother wrote requesting she return home, she needed to attend a party in Mr. Stones's honor, but of course, Benjamin stayed behind. Isabella was sure Sir Andrew was interested in her friend. Sometimes Isabella wished to have been born a boy. Sighing she turned as Mildred came through the door.

"When is my mother coming home?"

"This afternoon; you have an appointment with Mrs. Arlington, the modiste, later today." Mildred handed Isabella a towel. "Seems you need new dresses."

Isabella took the cloth and dabbed her face watching Mildred. The maid turned, trying to look busy as she avoided looking at Isabella. A slow chill ran down her body.

"Mildred, what have you heard?"

The housekeeper fussed with some day gowns in Isabella's wardrobe, further avoiding looking at her. Isabella knew the action, Mildred knew something, she feared her brother was right, that her parents were angling for her to marry Mr. Stone. Her brother had warned her that's why she was being called home to attend the party for the gentleman.

"You know I cannot say, your mother has forbidden me talking about the party." Mildred pulled out a pretty muslin with blue trim. It matched her eyes but made her look too young.

Isabella held her tongue. It was no use for she did not want her mother's wrath to come down on the dear maid's head as well.

Mildred had been with them for five years, just before Isabella's first Season. The maid had been one of the few servants to remain, as her mother was a hard taskmaster and expected the help to perform several jobs for little pay. Mildred stayed and put up with her mother, doing the extra work of several servants including a ladies' maid for Isabella. Why she stayed, Isabella could only guess, but she trusted the maid to keep their conversations private and away from her mother's hearing. In fact, Mildred was the only one in the household she felt she could trust not to report her doings to her mother.

Mildred dressed her before going downstairs. Isabella picked up some sewing to keep her busy while she waited.

Isabella could hear her mother enter the house as she barked orders to the butler and then started in on ordering Mildred to some task.

"Has Isabella arrived?" Her mother's voice carried into the parlor.

"Yes, madam, she is in the parlor." Mildred's voice had an edge of sympathy.

Isabella tensed as the tapping of her mother's footsteps drew near, a familiar sound. Her mother swept into the room. "Good, you are home. We have an appointment with the modiste. I have your new wardrobe ordered. We just need to finalize the fittings. Do hurry Isabella, meet me in the hall. The carriage will be ready." Isabella's heart pounded as her mother left the room, as it always did when her mother had plans for her.

Isabella quickly retrieved her bonnet and cloak and settled on a chair in the hall so her mother would have no more complaints, Isabella hoped. She felt no better as they entered the modiste shop. Endless gowns were fitted while being poked and prodded with pins. Day gowns, walking gowns, evening gowns and, the worst of all, nightgowns made of the sheerest material, making Isabella blush to think of wearing them.

She dare not speak against the choices her mother made, although she felt they were a little too bold. Isabella accompanied her mother to the haberdasher where her purchases of gloves and matching reticules mounted, but her mother was still not done, they went on to the milliner's shop. Not once did her mother ask Isabella's opinion while picking out bonnets and trimmings. Isabella's jaw tightened while she bit her tongue, fisting the material of her skirt willing herself to remain calm.

"Isabella, you are wrinkling your skirt, what is the matter with you?" her mother scolded, giving her a firm stare.

"I am fine, I just see no reason for all these purchases." Isabella relaxed her grip, smoothing the folds of fabric on her gown.

"You will in due time." Her mother turned back to the clerk dismissing Isabella's concerns.

Isabella moved to examine some ribbons across the room. Did her mother think she was brainless or maybe she felt Isabella was naïve and could continue to be manipulated even though she had reached the age of majority several years ago?

By the time Isabella returned home, her mind was whirling, her suspicions had been confirmed. She didn't want to think about her parents' plans for her. Benjamin had to be right, Mother just ordered a trousseau which could only mean one thing... *marriage.*

CHAPTER 2

*C*olton Egerton paced the room, tapping the letter against his hand. How had this happened to his sister? She and her husband lived in India, where her husband worked for an import company. Now she was dead, and he had been left the guardian of her two daughters while her sons would remain in the company of their father. He understood his sister's concern that the girls be raised in England, where they could receive the proper training to become young ladies, but *him*? Colton Egerton, a bachelor? He had not planned on getting married for a long time yet.

He reread the letter. The girls were on their way and would be arriving within a fortnight at his country estate. Colton didn't even know what children needed, especially young girls! He slipped the letter into his breast pocket, running his hand through his chestnut hair. He knew he was in trouble. If there was a time to call in reinforcements, it was now.

He dashed off notes for his friends to meet him at the club and walked out the door handing the papers to his man, Digby. It was a short walk to Brooks where he settled down on a worn leather chair, drink in hand to wait. It turned dark as the evening waned, a man silently lit the lamps around the room while Colton closed his eyes for just a minute. Murmurs of gentlemen hummed around the room wafting with cigar smoke.

"Egerton, my gosh man, your note sounded urgent, but you look positively disheveled." Captain Charles Rutley settled himself into a matching chair across from Colton, concern etched across his face.

Colton lifted his tired eyes and slowly reached into his breast pocket, extracting the letter. He handed it across to his friend. Charles reached across, folding the letter into his hand and began to read.

He signaled a footman for another drink as he watched his friend read the letter from India. Charles handed Colton back the paper shaking his head. "It seems you'll be in charge of two young ladies. How old are they?"

Colton groaned as he reached for a new drink from the footman. Rubbing the cool glass along his forehead, he tried to wrap his mind around this new responsibility. He had assumed they were younger, but now he wasn't sure. "I have no idea. The letter doesn't mention their ages, and I haven't seen my sister in years. She was married and gone before I was out of the schoolroom."

"This must be serious, you look a mess, Egerton." Colton looked up into the face of his friend James Balfour, the Earl of Malmesbury. Silently he handed him the same letter. James sat next to Charles as he quickly read. Shaking his head, he handed it back.

"You see why I called you two here? I am at a total loss as to what to do. I don't even know how old the girls are." Colton took a long drink from his glass.

"Well, you're going to find out soon," said James. "The letter states they're coming to your country estate. It looks like you have two weeks to get home and open the place."

"You'll need to hire some staff and maybe a governess," Charles agreed.

Colton stiffened, his eyes wide. He didn't want to move back to the country, but he could see that his friends were right. His small bachelor apartment was no place to have two girls or young ladies. He cringed at the thought.

"Don't look so down, Egerton, I'll be back in the country this week and Rutley and I will help you through this. Besides, Susan knows what to do with children," James reassured him.

Susan? Colton rallied. Yes, he thought, the Countess of Malmesbury would know how to handle two girls. Colton began to relax.

It took a few days to vacate his rooms in London while his man Digby left ahead of him yesterday morning to get the caretaker started on opening the estate. It had been years since he'd been there. Colton wasn't sure what he would find, but he knew it would take a lot of work.

Colton had left for the war soon after his military training and hadn't been back to the country estate since. After his widowed mother died, the place was closed up. He missed her funeral because he was away fighting for England. His sister married long before he entered school and was living in India with her husband. He hadn't given it much thought after he returned to the continent.

He would soon be the ward of two ladies, him, a bachelor. Maybe they would be old enough to send off to finishing school. Isn't that what you did with girls? He would need to consult the countess.

Colton flexed his stiff hand. It ached since his war injury. The surgeon thought he would lose his arm, but it was saved by a young field surgeon. He'd received the injury defending his face from the assault of a French soldier. The sword had missed his eye but left a large gash along the right side of his face. He was lucky. His friend James intervened, taking the Frenchman's life before Colton lost his. He rubbed the long red scar running down his face. It no longer bothered him, thankful he was only left with surface wounds. Some soldiers came home with unseen traumas, but much more devastating to their families. He would live with his disfigurement and be glad of it.

He finished his business and left for James' townhome where he would be traveling on horseback with Charles and James back to the country.

The three men stood in front of Colton's country estate; his valet remained at the front entrance waiting for his master's instructions, James and Charles stood quietly by his side.

Colton shook his head. "I don't even know where to begin."

James gave Colton a slap on the back. "Do not despair until you have had a chance to take stock of the place. Come over tomorrow after you have had a chance to assess the needs of your estate. Then we will confer."

His friends left, and Colton slowly walked to the door approaching his man. "Is it as bad as it looks?"

"I'm afraid it's worse, my lord. The caretaker was drunk at the local inn. I managed to hire a few groundskeepers to start on the outside, trimming the brush away from the courtyard, but you'll need a housekeeper soon to hire the help needed. I am afraid it will be months before we see any progress."

Colton stepped inside where the air hung heavy and

dust danced in the light of the uncovered windows. His heart dropped at the sight of decay. It had been years since anyone lived here, he shouldn't be surprised, but he was.

"Well, Digby, let's take stock of the place and see where best to begin."

Read more on Amazon…

Made in the USA
Middletown, DE
23 August 2020

16120287R00120